AS
LONG
AS
IT'S
PERFECT

AS
LONG
AS
IT'S
PERFECT

A NOVEL

LISA TOGNOLA

SHE WRITES PRESS

Published 2019
Printed in the United States of America
ISBN: 978-1-63152-624-4 pbk
ISBN: 978-1-63152-625-1 ebk
Library of Congress Control Number: 2019906680

For information, address:
She Writes Press
1569 Solano Ave #546
Berkeley, CA 94707

Interior design by Tabitha Lahr

She Writes Press is a division of SparkPoint Studio, LLC.

All company and/or product names may be trade names, logos, trademarks, and/or registered trademarks and are the property of their respective owners.

As Long As It's Perfect is a work of fiction. Although some businesses, places and locales are real, certain characteristics have been changed. Names, characters and incidents are either the products of the author's imagination or used in a fictitious manner. Any resemblance to actual persons, living or dead, or actual events is purely coincidental.

To My Family

PROLOGUE: MY FIRST HOUSE

Downey, CA – October 1974

My first house was painted pale yellow. It had hardwood floors, a gabled roof, and exposed rafters that made it feel like a cottage. Inside, white cotton curtains sewn by my mother hung from two paneled windows on shiny brass rods. The furnishings were simple, yet comfortable—a pine kitchen table and chairs, painted white to match the curtains, and a rustic corner hutch that was taller than me—all handmade by my grandpa Gil, who worked at a furniture store. The furniture was perfectly proportioned to the scale of the house, which was no bigger than a tool shed and located in my parents' backyard.

My playhouse was a place where I could lift the latch to open the top half of the swinging Dutch door and say to friends, "This is my house, you can't come in"—and then, to their surprise, open the bottom half and let them in.

It was a place where I spent much of my childhood: throwing tea parties for my stuffed animals, crossing the threshold of my imagination, and playing out my fantasy of home. There in the shadow of my parents' house, standing at my Playskool kitchen rolling imaginary meatballs and cooking them in a lidded skillet, I created a magical world.

I can still feel the warm California sun peeking in through the door and kissing my eight-year-old cheeks. The Santa Ana wind blows in through the open windows as my pigtails swing side to side.

Outside, beyond a stretch of green grass, my grandmother, wearing a kerchief tied over her hair, is sweeping the patio with an old broom. She is humming in the distance. With my own miniature broom, I sweep my floor and brush cobwebs out of high corners, lost in the calm as I watch small clouds of dust float like fairies across the floor.

A sudden rattling sound startles me, the noise followed by an urgent "meow." I open the door. A black cat leaps inside; her paws land with a soft thump. Whiskers rubs against my bare leg, then slides her face along my hand as I pet her.

Normally, she spends her days exploring the neighborhood park behind our backyard.

"What if she gets lost and can't find her way home?" I remember asking my mother when Whiskers was a kitten.

"She'll always find her way back."

"But what if she wanders too far?"

"She won't," Mom said.

CHAPTER 1: FENCING WITH THE NEIGHBORS

Lexington Ave, Rye – June 2006

On a Thursday morning, the day of our house closing, Wim and I sat side by side in stiff leather chairs across from our attorney, Robert, in a conference room lined with scholarly, leather-bound legal books, the mood as serious as a British courtroom. Only this was Rye, New York, not Rye, England, and our attorney donned a suit and tie rather than a robe and wig.

Robert unfurled our house survey and tapped his finger on a dashed line that represented the fence that separated our yard from our neighbors'. "There's a problem," he said.

"What problem?" I asked. Problems worried me.

He peered at us over the top of his tortoiseshell reading glasses. "Your neighbors' fence is on your property."

Not only was it on our property, he said, it was four feet over the property line. Four feet was practically the depth of our entire yard at our old house, where relaxing out back meant sharing a hammock with your neighbor. In Rye, real estate was at such a premium that every square inch of land was valuable. I'd heard stories about backyards measuring several feet short and the whole deal falling through. Robert told us if we didn't move the fence, someday down the line our neighbors, the Zambonis, would have the right to claim it. "Squatters' rights," he said.

As I took in the news, my eyes drifted toward a painting of an English foxhunt, with hound dogs running chase and jumping a post-and-rail-style fence just like the one standing between us and our house closing.

Intellectually, I knew our situation was trivial: a wooden fence merely needed to shift over a few feet. But I was troubled by the notion that we hadn't even moved in yet and already had a potential Hatfield-McCoy feud on our hands. The last thing I wanted was contention with our neighbors. I glanced at Wim, who seemed vexed over having to cope with yet another house problem.

As desperate as I felt to avoid conflict with the neighbors, I was more desperate to close on this house. "I'll go to the Zambonis' tomorrow and talk to them," I said with more confidence than I felt. I didn't want to do it, but I felt I had to prove myself.

"You're sure?" Wim flashed me a look of surprise.

I nodded.

"I think that's the best approach," Robert said.

"Okay, then," said Wim as he picked up a heavy pen and reached for a small stack of papers on the table.

Watching him flip through the pages, I felt as if this moment were more than a house closing—it was a turning point in our lives. Buying this house was something I'd dreamed of our whole life together. Not *this* house, per se, but the perfect house. The house that would make our lives complete. For years we'd been wandering like nomads in the desert, and now we were on the verge of entering the Promised Land.

When we'd finished signing all the documents, Robert congratulated us and wished us luck—then reminded me that we still had a fence to muscle through.

•———•

The next day, I pulled into the driveway of our future home and headed straight to the Zambonis', feeling both determined and terrified. As I cut across the fresh-mowed grass, I noticed the trees bending in the wind and the birds circling overhead. A blackbird landed on the Zambonis' roof ledge, and as I watched it I admired the Palladian window arched over the front entry, which lent the house a prominent elegance. It was a strange fate that I'd pined over this very house ten years ago when I'd first dreamt of living on this street, and now I was standing on its porch looking next door onto my own new front yard.

I'd always wanted to see the inside of Sue Zamboni's house, though not under these circumstances.

A welcoming wreath hung on the front door, which I hoped was a good omen. I knocked and waited, half hoping that Sue wasn't home. It was ironic that my husband the businessman—accustomed to negotiating contracts, able to separate his emotions from his goals, to take opposition in stride—was sitting at work, drafting a banking agreement, while I, a stay-at-home mom whose greatest recent experience with conflict was centered on my son's refusal to eat broccoli, was about to "handle" this.

Sue, a petite, casually dressed redhead wearing a turquoise T-shirt and no makeup, swung open the door. "Hi, Janie! Come in, come in."

I looked at Sue, her fair skin and delicate features. With her perfect little turned-up button nose, she reminded me of Ariel from *The Little Mermaid*. By contrast, my tumbled mass of tobacco-colored curls and slightly askew nose were straight out of central casting for *Fiddler on the Roof.*

Sue smiled and ushered me inside. My eyes quickly moved past the foyer, surreptitiously taking in as much of the downstairs as possible. The large house, bright and airy and built only about a decade before the Zambonis had purchased it a few years earlier, had lots of big windows—a feature I hoped to emulate soon in our own home.

Sue and I had only spoken a few times at our children's school events, although Wim and her husband, Matt, were casually acquainted through their jobs and commute to Manhattan. I had always found her pleasant, and had noticed more than once how her kind eyes sparkled when she smiled—something I kept reminding myself of as I mustered the courage to bring up the problem fence.

The two of us made idle chitchat until she finally noticed the official-looking document that I was gripping so tightly it was beginning to wilt in my sweaty hand.

Sue leaned casually against her granite countertop as I bounced nervously on my toes. I rubbed my lips together, trying to quell my nerves.

"So, we found out that your fence is actually on our property . . ." I thought my bladder was going to give way. I actually looked down at my feet, hoping not to see a puddle.

"Oh, I'm sure it's not," she said. As the words rocketed out of her mouth, she looked out toward her yard as if seeing the fence from her window proved that it was in fact on her property. "I know, because when the fence company installed it they had a copy of the survey." She sounded so certain it was hard not to believe her. "Even the Adamsons approved the location."

I didn't have to be a psychic to read her mind: *You know, our old neighbors, the people you just bought a house from—that nice, easygoing couple whose kids used to run back and forth between yards, using the gate that we installed just for them—the ones who didn't cause problems.*

"Well, our attorney told us yesterday that it's on our property." I held up the wilted survey like a dangling question mark and watched her perfect eyebrows draw together in a frown that I could have sworn bore my initials.

"Let me see that." She snatched the limp document from my hand and scrutinized it under the pendant light over the kitchen island.

Finally, she handed back the survey, although, judging by the dark look on her face, what she wanted to do was shove it down the garbage disposal. Her arms, animated just seconds ago, were now crossed firmly over her chest. "I'll have to discuss this with my husband," she said distantly, as if I didn't know his name. Then she showed me out.

It wasn't winter, but I caught a frosty breeze as she shut the door.

•———•

"Maybe we shouldn't have said anything," I said to Wim the next morning as he dressed for work. He had just folded back the French cuffs of his shirtsleeves and was now, with practiced movements, running cufflinks—silver and mother-of-pearl—through their tiny holes, a feat that, like childbirth, seemed to defy physics. "We just bought the house and we're already making waves. Sue is probably complaining about us right now."

I imagined Sue speaking in hushed tones with her friends, nodding in the direction of our house. "Can you believe how petty they are?" she'd say. "What are they going to whine about next, that our grass isn't green enough?"

Wim stopped fastening his cufflink. "Janie, we had to say something, it's our property. I understand that it's a nuisance and an expense. But I'm sure if the shoe were on the other foot, she and Matt would have done the same thing."

"Do you think they'll dispute the survey? Do you think they'll try to sue us?"

"I think they'll move the fence," Wim said. "I can't talk about this any more right now, I need to get to work." He gave me a quick kiss as he strode past me in his navy pinstripe suit, looking confident and powerful. The opposite of how I felt.

•———•

The weekend passed. Nothing happened.

I convinced myself that Wim would have handled things more tactfully. I was sure that if he'd gone over there, Sue would have offered to move the fence immediately and then made him a cup of coffee.

I went to visit our new house every day, just to imagine what it would be like once we fixed it up and moved in. I dropped off my kids at school and then parked my minivan across the street so I could take in the tall trees and wide lawn that set off the house and surrounding landscape. I tried to avoid Sue altogether; I did not want another confrontation.

On Wednesday, five days after my visit with Sue, I heard a commotion in the backyard. I looked toward the Zambonis' driveway and saw a team of men moving their fence.

I called Wim at work.

"That's great," he said.

I wanted him to acknowledge my efforts and how difficult the whole ordeal had been for me, but it didn't seem to register. Instead, he said, "Now when the renovation starts, you'll be able to handle any construction problems that come up."

He was only half joking.

CHAPTER 2: LOVE ON A DOCK

Portugal – August 1988

"I told you, I'm not renting a car," Wim said.

"The girls are right," Max said. "Taking the bus to Sagres will take a lot longer."

"I don't care," Wim said sharply.

There was an uncomfortable pause, as if no one knew what to say next. I worried that Wim's stubbornness would undermine our plans to travel as a foursome—though the truth was, I wasn't sure I still wanted to.

Then Shayna asked Wim the question I suspected we were all wondering: "Why don't you want to rent a car?"

His mouth formed a thin, straight line. "I'm not traveling on my dad's credit card," he said, looking at me. Wim had worked all summer to earn the money to pay for his trip to Europe. My friend Shayna and I were being bankrolled by our parents.

"It's not that bad if we split the cost four ways," Shayna said.

Wim reached into his bag, pulled out a cigarette, and lit it.

"Well, you can do what you want," Shayna said to Wim. Then she looked at Max and me. "We're renting a car."

An hour later, Shayna and I sat wedged in the backseat of an old Citroën, Wim riding shotgun while Max, a cigarette pressed between his lips, steered us down winding alleys, through narrow cobblestone streets bustling with cafés, and past white bleached limestone buildings toward Portugal's Algarve.

Wim was sulking in the passenger seat, still grumbling to Max about money.

"What a jerk," Shayna whispered to me.

"I know," I whispered back. "He seemed so nice before." What had happened?

•——•

Shayna and I had met Wim and Max two days before in the American Express office in Madrid. Amid the buzz of Spanish speakers, we'd heard their American accents and introduced ourselves. The four of us had spent the afternoon together at the Plaza Mayor in an old-world Spanish tavern with dark wooden booths and warm brick walls, eating seafood paella loaded with crustaceans in a huge, flat pan and drinking pitcher after pitcher of fruit-filled sangria. Afterward, we'd grabbed more drinks at a loud and boisterous tapas bar, where Wim had parked himself next to me. We'd remained together for the rest of the evening.

Wim and Max had plans to travel to Portugal later that night, and Shayna and I were scheduled to arrive there two days later. They'd promised to pick us up at a train station in Lisbon.

"I think Wim likes you," she'd said encouragingly.

"I think I like him too," I'd responded.

But now I didn't know what to think.

Perhaps Shayna and I had been insensitive to his money concerns. Still, I hadn't liked how he'd lost his temper.

And yet I was charmed by his sense of authority. There was something alluring about the way he spoke his mind, the way he was unafraid to express himself.

"Max, your cigarette smoke is making me nauseous," Shayna said. She cupped her hand over her nose.

Max glanced in the rearview mirror at her and took a long drag of his cigarette. Then he exhaled sharply and flicked the cigarette out the window.

•————•

By afternoon we had reached Sagres, the rugged southwestern tip of Portugal, where the four of us spent the afternoon perched on the water's edge, nibbling on cream tarts, and watching the waves break against the shore.

From the shade of a café umbrella, I watched Wim sip espresso from a white cup so tiny it looked like a toy from a child's tea set.

At twenty-two, he could have passed for sixteen, with a lean body, a smooth chest, a youthful face, and short brown hair cropped like a shoeshine brush. I felt the urge to run my hand over his head and feel the soft prickle. There was something about the way he sat back in his plastic chair, one leg crossed over the other, taking long drags of his cigarette and observing his surroundings from behind aviator glasses. He was the kind of guy who could quickly identify a bluff in a poker game or hail a taxi with a commanding whistle. He reminded me a little of my dad.

I couldn't see his eyes, but I sensed he was staring at me from behind his dark glasses.

He finished his drink and reached out his hand to me. I followed him off the terrace and onto a steep, winding path.

"Where are we going?" I asked.

"You'll see."

There was a mystique about Wim that made me feel alive. The wind blew against our faces, and my heart pumped harder the higher we climbed.

When we reached the top of the ridge, I stopped to catch my breath. Wim slid his arm around my waist as we looked out at the horizon—a golden beach framed by dramatic, sea-carved cliffs. "This is the end of the world," he said.

"It's stunning," I replied, watching a tiny sailboat in the distance, seagulls soaring overhead, my body aroused by the warmth of his hand on my hip, the weight of it comforting and protective.

He drew me in and kissed me on the lips. Blood rushed through my veins, a surge of adrenaline that ricocheted through my body like a pinball in a machine, setting off lights, bells, and buzzers.

●————●

After Sagres, the four of us moved on to Lagos, where we witnessed live chicken races on the beach, watched our first bull fight, and were nearly trampled by an angry bull that had jumped the wall and entered the stands. Lagos is where Wim and I fell in love.

Our last night together, he and I sat side by side on the dock of a small marina, marveling at our chance meeting. The past three days had been a whirlwind of emotion that neither of us wanted to end.

"I don't want to leave," I said, looking out at the moonlit night.

Wim turned abruptly toward me. "So don't. Stay and travel with me."

"I wish I could."

"You can," he said. "Take a break from school. Sublet your apartment."

I shook my head, knowing I'd sooner fight an angry bull with my bare hands than disappoint my parents.

I leaned back into his arms and rested my head on his shoulder, gazing at the stars filling the night sky.

He turned me toward him, brushed my hair behind my ear, and then, cupping my chin, brought his lips to mine. His mouth was warm and tasted like tobacco—pleasantly masculine and sexy. My lips grazed his ears, small and soft. He groaned quietly and pulled me down onto the rough wood of the pier, stretching his body out next to mine. The hard surface beneath us didn't matter. His hand inched up to the highest reach of my thigh. My breath quickened as everything began to move faster, the heat rising between us until every point of contact felt like fire.

After we made love, we continued to lie there, lulled by the gently lapping water, our half-naked bodies dappled in light cast by the moon shining on the bay. Eventually, we fell asleep.

●———●

We awakened to the morning sun, our bodies cold and stiff. I struggled to my feet, the smell of seawater coming off the light breeze, the sky over the bay scattered with clouds. Wim lay beside me, gazing at the still water. I could feel that something had deepened between us, unspoken and powerful. It was as if we'd claimed new territories, like new stamps had been marked on our passports. Wim reached out his hand and cuffed my ankle, a single touch that sent a jolt through me. "Don't forget last night," he said.

What does he mean? That we're committed now? Or is this goodbye?

I hardly knew him, yet I couldn't stop wondering whether there was a future for us—whether I could see myself spending my life with him.

That night, I boarded the plane back to my home in California with a heavy heart, already feeling Wim's absence.

• ———— •

Three months after Wim and I said our goodbyes, I stood at my apartment mailbox, wading through bills and junk mail. There in the pile was a blue featherweight airmail envelope bordered in red, my name and address printed neatly across the front in black ink. On the back was his name, Wim Margolis, and a tiny heart with an arrow through it.

I smiled. Reading his letters was like getting a piece of him; other than our occasional long-distance phone calls, they were our only connection.

An elegant stamp adorned the envelope: Helvetia, the female national personification of Switzerland, in a flowing gown with a spear and a shield emblazoned with the Swiss flag.

I ran my finger under the envelope flap and slipped out two separate letters, four thin pages folded neatly into thirds. After several months of correspondence, Wim's handwriting had become familiar to me, a sophisticated blend of printing and script written in clean, confident lines.

My eyes flew across the page, but at the end of the second paragraph, I paused, grief-stricken. My backpacking boyfriend, who didn't speak a word of German, had just been offered a job at a major computer and electronics company in Switzerland.

He wrote:

I should be elated. Flowing with joy. Jumping up and down. Shouting. Getting drunk. Making love to you. And what am I doing? Pouting. Maybe I'm sad that so many miles separate us—that we can't be together—that it will be too long before I see you again. The holidays will be here before you know it. Don't forget Switzerland is calling your name. It's not really Switzerland, it's me, and I'm losing my voice. My dream has come true and I wonder if it is really what I want.

CHAPTER 3: KEEPING UP WITH THE EVERYBODYS

Raymond Ave, Rye – July 2005

O ne warm summer evening, sitting with Wim outside on our back deck, whispering so I wouldn't wake up the kids— their bedrooms were just above us—I brought up the idea of moving. It was an idea I'd been toying with for months, ever since my neighbor, realizing her cramped family room was too small to fit her three kids *and* her Christmas tree, had moved to a five-bedroom colonial with a family room twice the size of ours in nearby Rye Township.

The day she told me, I was sitting back in my lawn chair sipping coffee. I was so stunned by her news that I nearly dropped my latte. She'd been one of the holdouts, like me, who had stayed put while others sold their homes and moved to larger lots in the Township. I tried hard to smile. It's not that I wasn't happy for her. I knew that she and her husband had worked hard and made sacrifices. But so had Wim and I. And now I had to ask myself, *What's the point of working so hard if you don't have something to show for it?*

Later that day, I drove by her new house looking for flaws—ugly siding, an old roof, small windows. It's shameful to admit, but I was searching for any defect I could find to make myself feel better about my own house. Instead, what I saw was a handsome, two-story brick home with an expansive yard—a far cry from our small, plain-vanilla home on its matchbox lot. I drove home, fighting tears the whole way.

"Do you ever think about moving?" I asked Wim hesitantly.

"I thought you loved this house," he said. He was looking at the abundant azaleas blanketing the yard. It occurred to me that the luxuriant foliage in our flower garden was the only part of our home I still loved.

"I do. But we've lived here nearly ten years." I paused, thinking about the peculiar dream I'd been having lately, in which I suddenly discovered new rooms in my house that I didn't know were there. I wanted to feel like my home, a symbol of security and a wisely planned-out life, was enough. But I didn't.

While our home's four bedrooms adequately accommodated our family of five, we had a dearth of bathrooms. The tiny master bathroom was my only sanctuary, and our kids, ages four, seven, and ten, had recently begun to overtake it. Long gone were the days of luxuriating in a tub filled with lavender spice bath foam and breathing in the relaxing scent of lilac candles. Now I percolated in Fizzy Wizzies bath suds and massaged my body with heart-shaped My Little Pony finger-paint sponges.

This was not a home with marble countertops, crackling fireplaces, and a Juliet balcony. This was a launching pad to that home.

"This is not the house I picture raising teenagers in," I said. "Or the one I imagine having grandkids visit someday."

"You're thinking pretty far ahead," he said, talking to me as if I were a child.

"I'm just afraid if we wait too long it won't happen. We'll just keep talking about it and never do it and then we'll be stuck here, wishing we had. Doesn't it make sense to move sooner and have more time to enjoy a house while the kids are still young?"

I knew he didn't feel the way I did, but he at least seemed to be considering my point. Then he shook his head. "It's not a good idea right now. Housing prices are through the roof. Plus, if my career continues on this path and we stay put, I might be able to retire early."

"I understand," I said, although I didn't, not really. I wanted to maintain our current lifestyle, too—our yearly vacations, swim-club memberships, and dinners out. But not in this house.

•———•

In the weeks following that conversation—as I tripped over my children's school backpacks strewn across the living room floor, herniated a disk reaching overhead for the pancake griddle stored in our inadequate kitchen, and scraped dried poop off my bird-bombed minivan because we didn't have a garage—I realized this was a dream I could not let go of.

We had tried to buy more time in our house by giving it numerous face-lifts, including an updated bathroom and a remodeled basement. As the years expanded, so had the house. We'd stretched it to its full capacity, until every square inch of the lot coverage was maximized. Further growth was not an option.

Lately, I'd resorted to magic, employing the oldest trick in the book: mirrors. Round mirrors, square mirrors, oval mirrors—I hung them everywhere short of my bedroom ceiling (much to Wim's chagrin). They didn't add much, however, except for a carnival fun-house effect that delighted my seven-year-old and the fin-gerprint smudge–leaving playmates he frequently brought home, crowding our already bursting-at-the-seams house even further.

Even after all that, during a first-time playdate, one young school friend, at the end of a quick tour of our home, asked, "Where's the rest of your house?"

I didn't know whether to laugh or cry.

CHAPTER 4: WHERE IN THE WORLD?

Raymond Ave, Rye – October 2005

It took time, but I eventually wore Wim down. Maybe the countless HGTV shows I subjected him to were what did it. I'd become addicted to the channel, obsessed with home building and design. My guilty pleasure was *House Hunters*, a show that followed prospective homebuyers as they toured three properties for sale. The end of the episode showed the new homeowners all settled inside the house they'd selected, living happily ever after. It always triggered my own yearning for that ideal nesting place of pleasure and security. Whenever Wim watched with me, I prayed it would work its magic on him too.

I watched and rewatched an episode featuring a second-floor linen closet that was larger than my entire kitchen. As the pangs sharpened, so did my complaints: "If we only had a mudroom, if we only had a garage, if we only had a larger kitchen . . ."

One night, when I opened the swelling pantry door and a sack of dog food fell on my head like a bowling ball, I finally put my foot down. "I've had it. We need a bigger house."

I knew Wim would be happy to remain curled up on the couch, reconciling the checkbook and reviewing his 401(k) in our little house, all of us crammed together like feet wedged in shoes too small. But for some reason he said, "Okay."

"Okay?" I replied. "Really? You mean it?"

"Sure," he teased. "Don't forget to send me your new address."

•———•

As we discussed our moving possibilities at great length, we began to formulate even grander ideas. We contemplated moving not just to another house but to an altogether different area of New York. Rye was an expensive place to live. We could spend the same amount of money and have waterfront property somewhere else.

"How about Larchmont?" Wim suggested. "I could still work in New York but come home each day to my private dock and take my boat out for a cruise."

Larchmont was beautiful, but I had searched the listings online and learned that there, as in Rye, the only water we could afford to live near was the local water treatment plant. So we broadened our scope to the rest of the country. We had always dreamed of South Carolina. Why save those white-sand beaches and eighteen holes of golf for retirement?

"How about Charleston?" I said.

"What about Roanoke, Virginia?" Wim said.

We even considered a place Wim's job had nearly taken us to four years earlier: Tokyo.

Seated at our favorite sushi bar in downtown Rye, we again debated the pros and cons of our current town over the delicate plucking sounds of a Japanese zither. Wim carved out a chunk of green wasabi from the small mound on his plate with a chopstick and stirred it into his soy sauce, turning it a muddy gray.

"Maybe now's the time to move to Japan," I said. "The kids are older and the transition would be easier." I still wasn't certain how Wim felt now, four years later, about the job offer he'd declined in Tokyo. I searched his face for a sign. He was unreadable. I knew better than to ask him. Not only was my husband not outwardly contemplative; he didn't like to talk about pesky things like feelings. Sitting here now, watching him dip a piece of yellowtail into the murky goo in the dish in front of him and pop the bite-size morsel into his mouth, I sensed his disappointment that we hadn't moved abroad when the opportunity had presented itself.

Suddenly he was coughing, a fit so relentless I feared he might fracture a rib. I pushed a glass of water toward him but he shook his head and waved the glass away.

I waited for the coughing to subside. "You look like you just swallowed fire," I said.

He cleared his throat and dabbed tears from his eyes with his sleeve.

"This really is a great area," I said. Bolstered by my own enthusiasm, I started to list all the things that had brought us to Rye in the first place: the twenty-five railroad miles into Manhattan; the excellent public schools; the town's pride in balancing modern amenities with old-world charm; the quaint brick library in the center of town; the cute shops lining the downtown streets.

"We pay the price for all that," he reminded me.

"But they're all the things that are important to us," I said, reminding him of the historic architecture, the occasional sighting of backyards dotted with laundry strung on lines with clothespins—hallmarks of a bygone era.

I looked out the window and across Main Street to the local watering hole, Ruby's. Next door were the peppermint-like swirls of Frank's Barber Shop, where Anna, a Russian hair stylist with a thick accent, cut Wim's hair each month, and Blooming Nail Salon, where I occasionally treated myself to a manicure. These were the kind of mom-and-pop establishments that created a feeling of belonging for me.

I watched a ponytailed woman take her daughter's hand and shuffle across the street to Arcade Booksellers. Gazing at the woman—dressed in crisp tennis whites and a matching white cap, her freshly manicured, cherry red toes separated by strips of fuzzy cotton and poking out of disposable paper sandals—it occurred to me how fortunate we were to live in what used to be a summer resort town and now felt like daily resort living.

Despite its wealth, Rye had a low-key feel about it. There were a few high-end restaurants, but no ritzy hotels. Most people were community oriented. Every summer, our street held a potluck-style block party where dads manned the grills, moms chased after toddlers, and kids rode bikes in the street. One summer, we roasted a pig on our front lawn. This neighborliness was a delightful but foreign concept to a girl from Los Angeles, where competition and self-interest run amok.

But it wasn't perfect. Many people in the community were conservative and conventional, with values and beliefs that differed from mine. I brought that up now.

"Listen, no place is going to be perfect," Wim said. "The kids are settled here. We've made close friends. I don't know why we keep thinking about somewhere else. We live in a really nice town."

"You don't have to convince me," I said. But by this time, we both needed convincing. I had planted the seed that we deserved more. This was 2005: Jobs in finance were relatively easy to get, and the economy was booming. We had choices. We could pretty much live wherever we wanted, as long as it was near a large financial district. The problem with having so many choices was that we couldn't feel satisfied with our current state because we were always thinking about what was next. In our endless pursuit of happiness and success, we tortured ourselves with the thought *Could our lives be better someplace else?* We were bent on finding just the right setting, just the right house. We thought this would fulfill our fantasies of having it all.

How ironic that after considering cities the world over, we ended up right back where we started.

CHAPTER 5: HERSHEY'S BARS

Downey, CA – September 1974

D r. Sosa's office was bright and airy. The reception desk held a bowl of candy—not the butterscotches and fruit-filled hard candies that Grandma kept for her mahjong group, but the real deal, mini Hershey's and Nestlé Crunch bars, the kind of sweets my parents allowed only on Halloween.

Every week Dr. Sosa and I sat together at a small table in her office, and she pointed to a shelf stacked with board games and puzzles. "What would you like to play today?" she asked.

My answer was predictable: "Mousetrap."

Although only in her sixties, Dr. Sosa seemed ancient. She wore her short red hair layered, and she reminded me, with her shriveled but kind face, of an apple-head doll. Together, we'd unfold the cardboard game board and lay out the plastic pieces— the blue and yellow assembly parts, the smooth metal ball, the die, and the colorful mice. Piece by piece, we'd build a trap.

Why was I drawn to that particular game? Perhaps it was the challenge of building something tangible that I could control; it lent a sense of order. Maybe it was the excitement of the unknown, the thrill of competition, and the triumph of winning. Maybe it was the way the pieces came together in one assembled unit when I turned the crank to start the mousetrap, booting the marble down the chute, propelling a plastic man into the air, and releasing the trap to capture the mouse.

I didn't know what separation anxiety disorder was, or what a clinical psychologist did, exactly, but I trusted that this nice apple-head lady who played games with me and gave me candy each week would make me better.

●———●

My childhood was not trauma-filled. But there is one incident I still recall in vivid detail.

It happened the summer I turned eight. We were at a beach in Boca Raton, Florida. The wind was kicking up, and people were folding chairs and umbrellas and gathering their belongings.

"Kids, let's pack it up, it's getting windy," Mom said.

I nodded, barely looking up from the arched double door I was carving into the sand.

"Janie, honey," she said. "Let's go."

I looked up from the sand. "But it's not done." I was building a fortress with a turret and four protective walls.

"We need to get cleaned up for dinner." She picked up the last beach towel, shook out the sand, and tucked it under her arm.

"Can I stay a little longer?" I sat there, waiting to see if she'd say yes.

She paused. She looked toward the hotel, and then back at me. I could tell she was considering it.

"Please, Mom?"

"All right, you can stay ten more minutes. But then come straight back to the room."

"Okay." I smiled; I couldn't believe she'd said yes! "I will."

My castle needed one last accessory. A mother-of-pearl seashell caught my eye. It would make a perfect door. I picked up the mollusk and filled in the missing piece.

Not wanting to watch my carefully crafted castle succumb to the tide, I stood up to leave—and, with a sudden, sickening drop of my heart, realized that I didn't know our room number.

I frantically scanned the beach, searching for my parents, though I knew they were back at the hotel. As I looked around I saw only strangers—kids carrying plastic buckets and dragging their towels behind them, their parents prodding them along. *How will I find them?*

The concierge found me wandering through the hotel lobby, red-faced and sobbing. He took me to the front desk and wrote some numbers down, and together we rode the elevators and proceeded to visit every Wolf registered at the hotel. There were four. It seemed odd to me that each time a guest opened the door, he said, "Is this your child?" instead of asking me, "Is this your parent?"

My parents' room was the last door he knocked on.

I never discussed this incident with Dr. Sosa.

• —— •

With each move forward with my mouse, I worked on learning coping skills. After weeks of taking baby steps toward independence and accomplishing such goals as visiting friends for longer and longer periods of time (for a reward: a new toy each week and the promise of a kitten at the very end), I started to feel better.

When my mother said, "I will always come back," I started to believe her.

Eventually, I stopped going to Dr. Sosa. The only thing I missed was the Hershey's bars.

CHAPTER 6: FINDING LEXINGTON

Raymond Ave, Rye – October 2005

I handed our real estate agent, Betsy, a list of criteria that eliminated any homes situated near power lines, double-yellow-lined streets, or public buildings. "Just to warn you, Wim and I are kind of finicky," I'd told her the first time we met.

"I've been in the real estate business for thirty-five years," she answered. "Don't worry, I've seen it all."

Betsy wore her brown hair in a pageboy style, only instead of the bangs being blunt they were lightly feathered away from her face—practical, professional. Although a born-and-raised New Yorker, she seemed to have a Midwest sensibility: proud, hard-working, the kind of woman who went about her business without much fanfare or drama. She wore sensible shoes and called soda "pop." I imagined her living in a house with a wide porch decorated with potted geraniums, situated amid endless fields of corn.

We weren't looking for a Rockefeller estate. All we wanted was a slightly larger home with modern amenities like a two-car garage, a kitchen island, and a mudroom. We wanted an easy commute to Manhattan and good schools. Okay, maybe we did want it all. But no more so than anyone else did.

A few days after our initial meeting, she called us. "I've got one I think you'll really like." She read the listing to me out loud: "Magnificent four-bedroom, three full baths, newly renovated kitchen, beautifully landscaped property, and more."

There's gotta be a catch, I told myself. *How can a house in our price range be that perfect?*

The next day, I found myself moving, sleuth-like, through the newly renovated colonial, waiting, wondering when the major defect would rear its ugly head. I made it through the house pleasantly surprised. Then I stepped out to the backyard. A five-hundred-foot tall industrial water tank, painted green, towered over the backyard like the Jolly Green Giant, dwarfing the house that had looked mansion-like just minutes before.

Some version of this happened at house after house. Everything would look good until, bam, we'd discover a problem with location or layout—problems that could not be fixed with a hammer and nails.

We decided to focus on streets instead of houses, figuring we couldn't change geography but we could always alter a house. Country lanes with rambling homes charmed me. Wim preferred prim-looking streets with more conservative colonial homes. We scanned every neighborhood in our zip code. We surveyed territory on foot, by car, and via satellite. Wim had become obsessed with Google Earth and the spy superpower its sophisticated technology lent him. With the click of a mouse he could observe properties from fifty thousand feet above sea level. An aerial view of what looked like a shoebox from the sky enabled him to assess the property in relation to its surroundings: its proximity to other homes, schools, and Ruby's, which was our favorite eatery. Sizing up our neighbors' lots became a full-fledged spectator sport.

"What kind of real estate espionage are you up to now?" I asked one evening, glancing over Wim's shoulder.

"See for yourself," he said.

"What?" I leaned in closer to the screen. My eyes widened at the words Wim had just typed. "Spying on my wife and enjoying the view . . ."

He laughed and drew me onto his lap. We exchanged a warm kiss, and then I placed my hands on the keyboard and typed, "The view's better in the bedroom . . ."

•———•

If our criteria weren't already strict enough, the more we scrutinized every street, road, lane, and alley in Rye, the more our differing personal preferences became apparent. Ultimately, a *Green Acres* dilemma ensued, where I was the pitchfork-bearer who longed for a bucolic setting and Wim was the slicker, pining for the city. Nothing fit the bill: it's too rural; it's too crowded; it's too close to town; it's far too remote. How could we ever find a house if we couldn't even agree on a street?

Then Lexington Avenue emerged. I had driven up Lexington Avenue many times over the past ten years and dreamt of owning a home somewhere along its long, gently winding, oak tree–lined road. On my fantasy drives, I would cruise its hilly surroundings, reminiscent of the neighborhood where I grew up, envisioning a life there.

Lexington Avenue offered a glimmer of city, with its pedestrian hustle and bustle and proximity to town, and also the wooded flavor of the countryside. Its Cape Cods, colonials, and Tudors were varied and unique, and widely spaced but close enough to borrow a cup of sugar. It was a wider street than most; many of the houses were on park-like quarter- to half-acre lots, immense by Borough standards. And larger properties meant larger setbacks, so the houses of Lexington Avenue stood gracefully behind expansive green lawns that lent a sophisticated air to the street. The houses were big—many in the three thousand to four thousand square foot range—but they weren't forbiddingly grand. They were simple, classic, and refined.

All of these features made the street special. They also made it sought after. "We couldn't afford a tree house on Lexington Avenue," Wim told me early in our search. For many, the street was untouchable, which is why we had eliminated it from our house hunt to begin with. "Homes rarely come on the market on that street. Many families root in and stay for a lifetime," Betsy had said during our first meeting, prompting a sudden flashback of me as a young girl, standing inside my little yellow playhouse and telling my friends, "You can't come in." Now I was the one being shut out.

Perhaps simply *because* houses on Lexington Avenue were out of our reach, we wanted more than ever to live on that street.

•———•

Betsy was driving me up Lexington Avenue in her gray Honda CR-V and supplying me with background information on two homes that had just come on the market. Still marveling at our stroke of good luck, I struggled to turn off my mind's chatter: *What did Betsy say? A divorce? A relocation? I wonder where the owners are moving. Is there someplace better that I don't know about?* I tried to capture every last detail to share with Wim when he returned home from work. I leaned in, straining to hear Betsy's every word, as if this were a military mission and my life depended on it.

"The street is unique in that, like the town, it's divided," Betsy was saying as she dropped her visor to shield her eyes against the bright October sun streaming through the trees. "There's lower Lexington and then upper Lexington, where the street becomes one-way."

And, I noted to myself, *where the houses become much larger*.

Betsy continued up Lexington at a frustratingly casual pace; I had to suppress the urge to thrust my body forward in an effort to gain momentum, to accelerate the car beyond snail speed. Just about the time I was considering opening the door and running to the first house I saw with a FOR SALE sign, she pulled up to a pretty colonial.

Within minutes, I could see that it wasn't for us. It was old. It was cramped. We could get that by staying in our current house.

We moved on to the next house, but there too I only needed one glimpse. It was old. It was cramped. And for what they were asking, we could buy a fantasy island in the New Zealand Marlborough Sounds, complete with house, two beaches, and our own private ecosystem.

●———●

"Do you think we're being unreasonable?" I asked Wim a few months later as we got ready for bed. We'd just seen and rejected yet another cramped house that had come on the market on Lexington Avenue. "We went from considering the entire Eastern seaboard and Japan to obsessing over a single street. What if the right house never comes on the market? There are only so many houses on one street. We could wait forever."

"It won't be forever."

"Should we branch out a little?"

"I'm not living in the Township."

"Well, what about Elmhurst? That's in the Borough."

"We're going to live on Lexington Avenue," was all he said.

I smiled inside, moved by his sudden resolve to pursue our dream location. But as I thought about the odds stacked against us, my smile faded.

•————•

I'd just come off a Costco run and was standing in my kitchen, contemplating where to store the giant packages of Bounty piled on the countertop, when I noticed the blinking red light on our answering machine. I pressed the button.

"Betsy here. There's a house that's come available on Lexington Avenue. It's just what you've been waiting for."

We'd been house-hunting for eight months.

•————•

The distance from our current home on Raymond Avenue to the house on Lexington Avenue was only two miles, but my eagerness to get there made it feel like light years passed before Betsy stopped the car in front of a white Cape Cod.

"Here we are," she said.

I let out a wistful sigh. It sat like an old shelved book, waiting to be taken down and blown free of dust.

I was smitten with the house immediately, but what impressed me even more was the location. It was close enough to the street to feel connected, yet far enough back to feel protected. The house sat partially hidden behind an ornamental tree wider than it was tall, its low, spreading branches offering a spectacular display of creamy white, star-shaped flowers. My mind drifted back to memories of the dogwood trees my dad used to point out on our walks.

This time I didn't bound out of the car and sprint to the door. I remained seated for a moment, taking it all in, imagining myself pulling into the driveway each day, coming home to all this.

Betsy punched in the code on the lock box, and I thought about how many times I had stood in this same position, waiting, hoping for the right house. All the places I'd seen suddenly blended together into a single generic house, like the green plastic buildings I'd collected playing Monopoly as a child. I bounced impatiently on my toes as Betsy turned the key and led me in the front door.

My heart dropped a little when we entered a dark foyer with a ceiling so low my ten-year-old could have touched it. The six-foot ceiling carried as far as I could see.

Keep an open mind, I reminded myself. But the farther in I got, the further my mind squeezed shut. Outdated dark wood paneling lined the den walls. The kitchen had been frozen in time since the 1970s. I cringed at the dull laminate cabinets and old Formica countertops.

"The kitchen could use some updating," Betsy was saying, "but the house has good bones."

The house was literally skeletal, void of furniture, as the owners had already moved out of state for a new job. Vacant and soulless, it was nothing but a shell, reminding me of my children's hermit crabs, who shed and abandoned their too-small casings before moving into new, larger ones.

Upstairs the only sign of life were pigs, litters of them, on wallpapers, shower curtains, and cabinet knobs. "Looks like the owner had a penchant for pigs," Betsy said—but beyond that, there was little more she could offer. It was a standard four-bedroom house with outdated bathrooms and no architectural interest.

Except . . . "Oh, wow," I said, looking out the window of the master bedroom. There was a magnificently tall, high-branching beech tree—stout trunk and smooth, silver-gray bark that glistened in the sun—just outside. But it was what was behind the beech that really made me gasp. Stretching in both directions was a wooded hollow—layers of trees, giant oaks that looked like they'd been there since Adam, stretching as far as the eye could see. The landscape was lush and green and fertile and gave the impression of being wild.

Betsy walked up and stopped next to me. "There's a dell back there that runs down the entire length of the street."

As I stood, gazing at the vista, I couldn't wait to bring Wim to see it. "I think Wim is going to love it," I said.

•———•

The next morning, a Saturday, Wim and I lay in bed, already discussing the house. While we had mulled over the idea of moving for months, it hadn't seemed real until now. Here was a home for sale in an ideal location. One we could remodel and customize to suit our lives.

I got up and looked out at the big oak that shaded our bedroom, wanting to open the windows to let in the breeze. The noise from the Department of Public Works, located just behind our house, made me keep it shut.

"Think about all the features we've dreamed of having—a Jacuzzi tub, a huge shower, a master bedroom fireplace, a big walk-in closet," I said. "It would be like being in a vacation home all the time. Can't you picture yourself putting your suit on in the morning in a spacious area instead of the tiny space you have outside your closet now?" More space would be good for our kids, our minds, our marriage.

He nodded. "It would be nice to have a closet deep enough that I don't have to smash my dress shirts to close the door."

"Yeah, one of those big dressing areas like the ones you see in magazines, with closets that look like furniture. And built-in shoe racks."

"We could have a big ottoman in the center where I could sit down and put on my shoes," he said.

"I can just picture you sitting on a leather ottoman under a sparkling chandelier, surrounded by mahogany closets, putting on your fancy Italian shoes," I said, relishing our shared fantasy. "You deserve it, you know." And I meant it. I gave him a look of admiration and appreciation. A look that, I knew, I didn't give him often enough.

• —— •

"Can we really afford this house?" I asked later that day, attempting to be practical.

"The price is ridiculously high. And we'll have to do a huge remodel." He frowned.

I braced myself for disappointment and waited for him to hand over the bad news.

"But I think it's worth the investment," he said.

My heart danced a little jig. "Are you sure?"

"If anything happens to my job, we could manage here without any dramatic changes to our lifestyle. We're giving up that security by moving."

It was an honest answer, but not the one I'd hoped for.

"We don't have to do this," I said. But deep down, I knew we did. Never mind that he'd expressed reluctance from the beginning, that he prioritized financial security over spacious living. I'd convinced myself that this move was necessary for all our sakes.

CHAPTER 7: READY FOR TAKEOFF

Rosemead, CA – December 1994

Wim told me his news over steaks at Clearman's North Woods Inn, our special-occasion restaurant, though he hadn't yet revealed the occasion. The steakhouse was a favorite of ours, built in log-cabin style with dark wood reminiscent of the Swiss Alps. There was even fake snow covering the roof.

"I was waiting for the right time to tell you," he said.

I scooted my chair in closer. "Tell me what?"

"Morgan Stanley's closing the LA office. They've offered me a job in New York."

New York? My mind started racing. I pictured throngs of people fighting their way down littered sidewalks, taxi drivers honking their horns relentlessly.

"Are you really considering taking this job?"

"I *am* taking the job."

I didn't even know where to begin. Other than New York, I had only a vague notion of the East Coast. It was a seventh-grade civics lesson on Pilgrims and Plymouth Rock. It was a bunch of old states with a few that happened to begin with "New." It was where the ocean was Atlantic, not Pacific. It was home of the Boston Massacre and witch trials. I felt suddenly out of breath.

"But the timing . . . we had everything timed just right," I said, placing my hand on my stomach.

The baby was due right after I graduated, just as Wim and I had planned.

Life is full of surprises, I thought, watching the couple next to us eat peanuts and throw the shells on the floor, a popular Clearman's custom.

"We don't have to live in the city," Wim said, as if he were doing me a favor.

"We haven't even discussed this and you're already talking about where we'll live?"

Wim's new job would be located in the heart of the most exciting city on earth and the financial capital of the world. He would be working in a skyscraper, chasing his fortune and feeling as tall as the Empire State Building. He was ecstatic. This was his ticket out of LA.

As for me, after three months, my morning sickness had finally subsided, but now I felt as though I were carrying a sack full of sand in my belly. My heartburn had become worse. My breasts were tender, my feet swollen. I had pelvic cramps. "It's just your uterus growing," Wim would say, the two of us sitting huddled over a dog-eared copy of *What to Expect When You're Expecting*.

"What about after the baby is born? What about my family?" I shifted on the plush leather banquette and instinctively rubbed my hand over my belly in a slow, circular motion, trying to imagine raising a child without my family nearby.

We paused our conversation while our waitress, dressed in a barmaid costume, rolled a cart topped with a grill over to our table, the wheels crunching over the peanut shells scattered along the ground.

She splashed some brandy and lit a long match and suddenly the grill erupted into a small inferno; I could feel the heat through my sweater. She transferred the sizzling steaks to our plates, then reached over me and opened my gigantic potato, spooning in hot au jus, whipped butter, sour cream, chives, and cheese sauce. "Enjoy your meal," she said before shimmying away with the cart.

Wim stared at the enormous rib eye that took up three quarters of his plate. "Don't worry. It's not like you'll be alone. I'll be there. And we're going to have family around, too: my parents, my sister, my brother, Gram . . ."

I loved Wim's family. They always made me feel special. And I knew they would help as much as they could—but still, they weren't a replacement for my own family.

I thought of my grandma Rose, my mom's mom, and our weekly dinners at her small apartment—located a stone's throw from my parents' house—where she always served the same baked chicken or meatloaf, a stuffed potato, and string beans, simple but delicious. She could spend a half hour at the grocery store just picking out the best-looking beans. "*Setz. Essen,*" she'd say. ("Sit. Eat.")

There was a roughness to Grandma Rose, like an unpolished gem, but also an underlying tenderness and affection. As a child, I'd sat with her at her dining room table and she'd patiently taught me Russian poetry by Pushkin, reciting the lines phrase by phrase and prompting me to repeat them until I had the entire poem memorized, much in the same way my mother sometimes taught me Yiddish words Grandma Rose had taught her.

Dessert was two homemade brownies cut into squares—or, as my grandma pronounced them in her strong Russian accent, "skvehs."

She often stared into my face, sipping tea from a plastic teacup, a single sugar cube bulging from the inside of her cheek, and said, "You look a little like my sister Sonja." How would I know? I had never met any of her siblings. My grandma had left her homeland after giving birth to my aunt Fran, eight years before my mother was born. She left behind her parents and six siblings to follow her husband to America in order to escape the oppressive environment in Russia before the war. A few years later, her entire family was murdered in the Holocaust. She'd lived with the guilt of leaving, and of surviving, ever since.

There was no comparing our situations. I did anyway. Now I, too, would be leaving my family. *Who will stroll my kids at the park? Who will help them memorize Russian poems? Who will teach them Yiddish phrases? Who will squeeze their cheeks with love, call them* Dova'leh, *and feed them See's candy?*

Wim picked up his fork and serrated knife and cut into his thick steak. "Maybe this will be good for you."

I folded my arms over my stomach. "What do you mean?"

"You've always been so dependent on your parents. You've said so yourself." He always raised his eyebrows when he knew he was right.

I thought if I didn't say anything, he might drop the subject. I was wrong.

"Janie, your dad still takes you to get your car washed," he said.

"That's his way of showing me he cares." I pictured my Dad and me sitting side by side on a tree-shaded bench at the Downey Carwash, sharing a vending machine Coke and watching the conveyor belt guide my white Datsun through the long, tunnel-like bay on its way to get soaped, rinsed, and waxed.

"So when he takes you to get your car fully detailed every year, he's simply professing his love and devotion?"

"That's right," I said.

"How about when you returned that red dress you bought at Nordstrom last week because your mom decided it was 'garish'?"

"It *was* garish," I said indignantly, my defenses rising.

He closed his eyes. "I'm not trying to make you feel bad," he said gently. "My point is, maybe this will help you learn to make decisions for yourself without always needing their approval."

"Maybe," I said.

• ——— •

The following weekend, we settled down at my parents' kitchen table. Morning sunlight streamed through the oversize window; outside, a hummingbird fed from a tall bird of paradise, its flower stretching out like a bird's beak, its orange and deep blue petals fanning into a crown, giving the flower the appearance of a crane. The hummingbird's flapping wings reminded me of the fluttering I was beginning to feel in my stomach—partly from our baby's movements, and partly from my own racing heartbeat as I prepared to deliver my parents news that would change all of our lives forever.

My parents were dressed in their bathrobes, the *LA Times* strewn across the table: the business section splayed out before my dad, Metro in front of my mom.

"So, to what do we owe the pleasure of this visit?" my mom said. She slid a bowl of cantaloupe in front of Wim. "Try it, it tastes just like sugar."

Although we'd just eaten breakfast at our apartment, Wim graciously popped a hunk of the drippy fruit into his mouth.

As he wiped his chin clean with a napkin, I shook my head no thanks. Wim gave me an encouraging nod. Taking his cue, I said, "We have some good news and bad news." I watched the steam rise from my father's cup of Sanka. He held the mug, filled to the brim, with two hands, lifted it carefully to his lips, and took a small sip. As he did, he and my mom shared a glance across the table.

"Let's hear the good news first," my mom said.

"Okay," I said. "The good news is that Morgan Stanley is offering Wim another job—"

"That's wonderful!" my mom blurted.

"Congratulations, Wim!" my dad said with an emphasis on "Wim," a quirky habit of his that made me smile; it was as if he thought emphasizing a person's name validated the hard work that had gone into whatever achievement they were celebrating.

My dad had always said that Wim had a good head on his shoulders, and I'd been grateful to have my parent's blessing when we'd married. "Marry a man who will take good care of you," they'd told me many times—words that had always made me feel conflicted. On the one hand, I knew they only wanted the best for me. On the other hand, I'd always felt that they thought I needed taking care of—that, unlike Wim, I couldn't manage on my own.

They both smiled at Wim and then turned their gazes back to me, looking at me expectantly.

"Now let's hear the bad news," my dad said quickly, a trace of apprehension in his voice.

My palms started to sweat. I was nervous, yet deep down, I knew that part of me was enjoying this. As the youngest in my family, as was typical of my birth order, I had often rebelled as a way of distinguishing myself from my older brother and sister. I was the risk taker, the one who'd always chosen a different path from the other members of my family. Sitting here with my parents, I thought of other times in my life I'd sat in this same chair and delivered surprising news: "Shayna and I plan to backpack through Europe for two months"; "I fell in love with a man who lives in Switzerland"; "Wim wants to move in with us." I thought about how each of those moments in my life had brought me to this point right now.

I glanced at Wim again. He was twirling his wedding ring in his fingers. Suddenly, I remembered Rabbi Eisenberg's wedding sermon about what our rings symbolized, how the hole in the center shouldn't be considered a space but rather a gateway leading to things and events both known and unknown. Now we would be entering that gateway; we were pioneers venturing into a new frontier, about to see what lay beyond the horizon.

I folded my hands on my lap and took a deep breath. "The bad news is . . ."

Wim looked up and gave me another encouraging nod.

"The job is in New York."

My mother's mouth dropped open. "New York? How long will you be there?"

"It's a permanent move," I said gently.

Tears welled up in her eyes. My father looked shaken but remained calm. Always stoic, he immediately launched into a speech about the importance of following one's career.

"But what about the offer you put in on that house in Manhattan Beach?" my mom was asking. "That corner lot with no backyard . . ."

"We didn't get the house," I said. An image came to mind of the four-bedroom, two-and-a-half-bath California ranch. It had been cramped and dated, and we'd lost it in a bidding war. In upscale Manhattan Beach—safe, smogless, good schools—even the most derelict houses didn't stay on the market more than a few hours. We hadn't really expected to win the bid. However, I *had* expected that our first home would be thirty miles away from my parents and not *three thousand* miles away.

I looked around my parents' kitchen as though it might be my last time. I remembered how the cabinets, now stained walnut, had once blended with the dark green exterior of the refrigerator and matching oven range, a color choice my mother came to regret a decade later. Back then, earthy shades were "in."

I recalled the wallpapered breakfast area, once bright with mod flowers in burnt orange and avocado green—the same wallpaper my brother Adam had once splattered with a fistful of spaghetti when our game of playful pea tossing suddenly escalated into a full-blown food fight. The paper had long since been stripped and replaced with neutral off-white paint. Now that my siblings and I were grown, food fights had been replaced with fits of laughter around the table— storytelling, poking fun, bathroom jokes—all of which I'd no longer be a part of.

The sound of metal hitting glass jolted me back to the present. Wim's ring had slipped from his fingers and fallen to the table with a loud clink. The thick band of gold vibrated against the glass surface until Wim clamped his hand over it and returned it to his finger.

"So the house hunt is over?" my mom asked.

"It is in LA." Part of me felt disloyal, as though I were betraying my entire family. "I'll fly home as much as I can. We're hoping you'll come visit us a lot."

"Of course we will."

"New York is the shopping capital of the world," I added.

"Actually, Janie's not going to leave yet, only I am," Wim interjected, explaining that he planned to start his new job the following month and that I would be staying back to finish my social work degree.

For the past several days, he and I had been mulling over our dilemma, asking ourselves how I could finish out my degree, and my pregnancy, without us being separated. I had considered transferring to a graduate school in New York so we could live together, but with only five months left, it made little sense.

"We wondered if Janie could stay with you until she's done with school," he said. "I'll be visiting as often as I can, but we thought it would be easier for her if she wasn't alone."

"Of course," my parents said in unison.

"She can stay as long as she likes," my dad added.

My first pregnancy was one of the most important milestones in our marriage, yet my husband wasn't going to be there to share it with me. Instead, my parents would play surrogate spouse.

"Don't worry, Wim," my dad said, reaching out and patting my head. "We'll take good care of her."

As I pushed my chair back from the table and stood up, it occurred to me that maybe Wim was right. Maybe at twenty-eight years old, it was time for me to stand on my own two feet. I knew that it would be good for me. I just didn't know that it would turn out to be harder than anything else I'd ever done.

• ———— •

Again, we were living apart, but this time we didn't write letters to each other; we were too busy, Wim with writing credit analyses for real estate deals, me with writing term papers for school.

Five months later, on a bright, cloudless, May day, I boarded American flight 2400 from LAX to LaGuardia, the last flight I'd take before our baby was born. Sitting on the tarmac, waiting for my plane to take off, I felt excited about what lay ahead yet torn up over what I was leaving behind. As I stared out the small oval window, I remembered how just a few days earlier, my mother had taken me shopping for maternity wear that would get me through my last month of pregnancy. "You can mix and match these shirts with the jeans or blue skirt we got you, and you'll have four new outfits," she'd said with the enthusiasm of a personal shopper.

I'd come home later that day to find my laundry folded in neat piles on my bed, courtesy of my dad, the same way he'd done since I'd moved back in with them. Soon, there would be no more folded laundry, no more outings to the carwash, no more walks together through the hills. There would be no more year-round sunshine and no more shopping sprees.

When the pilot announced that the flight would take an estimated five hours and forty minutes and that the weather in New York was currently "a cool 53 degrees with heavy rain," I quietly groaned. *What's worse*, I wondered, *the long flight ahead with this watermelon balanced on my bladder or the frigid temperatures awaiting me when we land?*

But the harsh weather wasn't the only thing I worried about. I'd never lived outside of LA, except for my time in college, and even then I'd been only two hours away. The idea that I would soon be entering another world where, other than Wim and his family, I wouldn't know a soul, was terrifying. To me, this move meant loss.

The engines spooled up for takeoff, and the seat belt sign went on. My heart fluttered. An announcement came over the loudspeaker: "We are ready for takeoff. Please make sure your seat belt is fastened and your tray is in an upright position." A passenger coughed. A baby let out a short wail. I loosened the blue nylon strap and extended it as far as it would stretch over my oversize belly.

I tried to lure my thoughts back to the idea of my new independence but found myself obsessing over all the birthday celebrations I'd miss, the weekly dinners with my grandma that would come to an abrupt end. I pictured my grandma squeezing me tight, our bodies rocking together from side to side, as we said our tearful goodbyes. *"Beris' druzhno, ne budet gruzno,"* she'd said—"Take hold of it together, it won't feel heavy"—reminding me that Wim and I would need to take care of each other.

As the plane sped down the runway, it felt like a buzz saw was reverberating through my chest. *Will being independent make me happy?* I wondered.

"Due to high winds over the Midwest, we are anticipating heavy turbulence in some areas, so please keep your seat belts fastened at all times when the safety light is on," the pilot warned.

I double-checked my seat belt buckle, closed my eyes, and prepared myself for the bumpy flight ahead.

CHAPTER 8: SMELLS LIKE POO

Raymond Ave, Rye – June 2006

As Wim and I sat side by side on plastic lounge chairs, legs splayed like untrussed turkeys, we took in the first rays of summer. We waved to our Raymond Avenue neighbors, Bonnie and Maurice Schreiber, who were home from their condo in Key West and playing Canasta with friends, their zinc-coated faces barely visible under wide-brimmed straw hats. Maurice had been a successful bank executive at Goldman Sachs. He and Bonnie lived in a modest colonial home with a small yard, drove practical Hondas, and belonged to the same casual swim club we did, the kind without a golf course or fancy dining room. The kind without a strict payment policy where if you're late paying the bill, you're forced to suffer either humiliation by public listing of your name for everyone to see or a stoning by martini olives. The kind where one hundred dollars buys you a membership, versus the local country club, where the same amount bought you a hot dog. Wim and I had lived next door to the Schreibers for the last eleven years and had always admired their restrained lifestyle. We prided ourselves on living the same way.

I remembered when the FOR SALE signs started popping up in our neighborhood, how Wim and I often privately pooh-poohed our neighbors' decision to move up to their dream home. Many were, like Wim, in the financial industry, an industry packed with distortions, the prize always moving just beyond your grasp. No matter how well you did, there was always someone doing better. You always had the feeling that, despite the fact that you were probably earning more than you ever dreamed you could, everyone around you seemed to be making more. It was a life-sucking industry, and yet we were dependent upon it.

We shook our heads and sighed when we heard that the Smiths, a young family who'd only lived in our neighborhood for four years, had just purchased a six-bedroom spec home with a heated in-ground pool and shuffleboard court in Rye Township. "They'll miss the kids cutting through each other's backyards to play . . . They'll miss being able to walk to the bagel shop . . . They'll miss their old mortgage payment when the new one doubles," we said. "Not us," we told each other. "We live within our means."

But over time, my feelings had changed from feeling proud to feeling left behind. I constantly wondered if I was missing out. What good did it do to live frugally when you didn't have a two-car garage and everyone else you knew did? In my mind, FOR SALE signs signaled happiness. To me, they said: *The Talberts are trading up to a French manor in the Hill Section with a three-car garage and a swimming pool, where they will be more fulfilled and successful,* and *The Labradas are moving to a five-bedroom colonial in the Township and pursuing something that you're not—novelty, adventure, and sumptuous living.* I knew I was confusing material success for actual happiness, but I didn't care. I was lusting for a more luxurious life. My dreams were growing too big, and I needed a place to put them.

It seemed everyone was either renovating their home or trading up—including, I suddenly realized, our siblings. Both our moms had dropped hints for years: "Maybe in your next house you'll have a mudroom, garage, laundry room . . ." and so on. Who could blame them? We lived in a culture built on improvements— characterized by relentless upgrades to cars, computers, appliances, and homes. We assumed that when something got replaced, the new item would be better.

Every time I learned about another family moving out of the neighborhood, I felt envy. I felt as if we didn't measure up, as if we were somehow less-than.

A skein of birds flew overhead, their loud calls marking the end of spring. "Look," Wim said, pointing to the sky. I looked up from my *House Beautiful* magazine and marveled at the perfect V formation in the sky. Dramatic, efficient, and simple—the same features we wanted for our new house.

We'd been searching and searching—had conducted numerous interviews, spent hours doing background checks, and reviewed references using a screening process worthy of Homeland Security. Yet we were no closer than when we'd started to hiring an architect.

"We're going to be spending a lot of time with this person, you especially," Wim had said when we started looking. "It's important that we find someone we have chemistry with."

With our remodeling project, Wim and I had assumed new roles in our marriage—roles I hoped would build more togetherness into our relationship. Other than a few part-time babysitters we'd had over the years, we'd never hired anyone together.

I turned to him, noticing how his skin, due to his usual defiant avoidance of sunscreen, had turned bright pink. "Do you remember the first architect we interviewed? That hippie with the ponytail and Birkenstocks? He was kind of out there, wasn't he?"

"Architects seem to march to the beat of their own drums," Wim said.

After the hippie, there'd been Bill, the guy with the impressive portfolio—a real charmer. But he'd reminded me of an ex-boyfriend who used to say, "Trust me," and then cheated on me.

Then there was the handsome and slick multimillionaire architect who'd pulled up to our house in a red convertible sports car. That had been a brief meeting, because once he'd told us his fee, we both knew that his Porsche was one of several we'd pay for by the time our house was finished.

I feared that if we couldn't find the right architect for the job, we'd be forced to design our house ourselves. I'd read those stories in home design magazines where a woman being interviewed says: "My husband and I started talking about it one day during our flight to Barbados, and before we knew it we had designed our entire two-story, ten-thousand-square-foot home on the back of a cocktail napkin!" But I knew that wasn't our reality. One, neither of us was particularly artistic. And two, with two mortgages to pay, we wouldn't be traveling to the Caribbean any time soon.

"I'm going in." Wim removed his sunglasses and rose from his chair.

I glanced up from my magazine, taking notice of my husband's body for the first time in months and realizing that I couldn't remember the last time I'd seen him undressed. Lately, I'd been focused less on body construction and more on house construction. I gazed at his broad shoulders, appreciating how his trim physique was silhouetted by the forest of trees in the background.

"You know where to find me." I reclined my chair and settled back into my magazine, back into my house-absorbed world. I flipped past sumptuous bathrooms with walk-in showers, elegant breakfast rooms with French doors, and droolworthy bedrooms with tray ceilings, gazing at the images with intensity, ogling the glossy spreads of dramatic entryways and exquisitely accessorized rooms layered with color and texture—surroundings of perfection. I took in a glamorous kitchen with crisp white cabinets, soapstone counters, and a metallic tile. I felt its warmth and luster, and it made me want to create my own *House Beautiful*—a desire so profound it made my blood surge. I hungrily tore out pictures from the latest issues of *Ideal Homes* and *Dream Kitchens and Baths*, knowing that soon, instead of fantasizing about designer rooms, I'd be living in them. All the pretending I'd done in my childhood playhouse had been a dress rehearsal for my life now, and the big moment was finally here.

Minutes later, Wim was standing over me, dripping water like a wet dog. His white legs stood out in stark contrast to his blue swim trunks.

"I was just talking to Jack Geller in the pool and he said his brother-in-law is an architect who does really detailed work," he said, wiping water from his face.

"Really?" I handed him a towel.

He rubbed his head and sat down next to me. "Jack gave me his phone number." He handed me a soggy scrap of paper with expanding ink.

I could just make out the blurry numbers. "I'll call him tonight."

———

The following Saturday, the doorbell rang at 9:00 a.m. sharp.

"Right on time. That's a good sign," I said to myself. I took a deep breath and opened the door to a tall man who looked to be about my age or slightly older. He wore a suit and tie—a nice touch, I thought, considering it was the weekend.

"Pleased to meet you." He extended his hand, and we shook.

His grip was firm and confident. I ticked another box on my mental checklist.

"Your newspaper was in your azaleas. I think your delivery boy could stand to improve his aim." He smiled and handed me *The Wall Street Journal*. With that, I was sold.

Wim and I led Luke into the dining room, and we all sat around the table. I noticed a pleasant mix of ease and formality about him. I also noticed an unpleasant odor emanating from his direction. It was a smell so pungent I half expected to see fumes.

Wim and I shared a confused glance but said nothing. I looked back at Luke and scrutinized him more closely. His clothes appeared clean. He looked freshly showered. So why did he stink?

I tried to ignore it and focus instead on Luke's questions about our project, the way he listened closely and nodded with understanding. Sitting there at my parents' old mahogany dining room table under the bright light of their old brass chandelier, I studied Luke's countenance, his squared jaw and well-proportioned features. Even his glasses were proportional to his face, which I saw as a good sign for an architect.

"I started out in construction, working summers for my uncle," he said. "By fifteen, I was doing everything: framing, drywall, painting." More recently, he'd worked for a reputable architectural firm and then branched out on his own. "Creative differences," he explained.

Observing his cropped hair, receding and speckled gray in customary forty-something fashion, I considered his bold career decision while trying not to inhale too deeply.

"There's one thing I should warn you about," Wim said. "Janie and I have a lot of our own ideas and want to be involved in every step of the design process."

I closed my eyes for a brief moment and imagined Luke high-tailing it out the door. When I opened them, he was still sitting there, looking unfazed.

"I enjoy having clients who know what they want," he said. I could feel his enthusiasm for the project as palpably as I could smell the foul odor permeating the air.

We wrapped up the interview, and as soon as we escorted him out the door I turned to Wim. "I really liked him! But . . . that smell!"

Wim agreed.

I walked back over to the table to realign the chairs and found that the smell was as strong as ever. There, behind Luke's chair, lay an enormous pile of fresh dog poo. Our Wheaten terrier, Copper, had seemingly picked this discreet location to do her business that morning. It was a miracle that Luke hadn't stepped in it on his way out.

He'd probably left our house thinking, *Nice people, but their house smells like shit.*

CHAPTER 9: LIPSTICK AND SPEED STICK

Downey, CA – September 1974

As a child, I welcomed the chance to spend time with my parents. I would accompany my mom on visits to her hairdresser or the butcher. One of my favorites was joining her when she went to see Mrs. Obermeyer, her dressmaker. We would pull up to her bungalow-style house and, as my mother gathered an armful of garments to be hemmed, I'd race ahead to ring the doorbell—a mechanical one with a lever that slid from side to side.

"Well, young lady, look how much you've grown!" Mrs. Obermeyer would say, her grandmotherly eyes twinkling behind thick glasses. Then she'd call off Sparky, her frantic Jack Russell terrier, and lead us into her spare bedroom, a tangled mass of sewing supplies and fabric bolts, a Singer sewing machine table in the corner of the room. My mom would stand in front of the antique floor mirror while Mrs. Obermeyer kneeled beside her, pinning up her hem. I would sit on the floor in a litter of fabric scraps, gazing up at a small collection of perfume bottles whose faceted glass sparkled across the oak dresser.

"What do you think, Mrs. Wolf, do you want the hem to fall below or above the knee?" she'd ask through her pin-filled mouth.

"Which makes my legs look longer?" my mom would answer, turning her slim body side to side.

•———•

Standing at the custom-built bar in the family room, my dad liked to prepare his daily after-work martini before settling into his mustard-yellow leather armchair to watch the six o'clock news. It was my job to fetch him two cocktail onions from the adjacent kitchen. I would carefully center and pierce the vinegary onion pearls onto a colored wooden toothpick. I had learned to respect my dad's reserve and would deliver his garnish with little fanfare. My reward came as an affectionate pat on the head before he returned to David Brinkley's evening update.

On occasion, just for the thrill of it, I'd steal a sip of crème de menthe from the crystal decanter my parents kept on the bar shelf, temptingly close to the Lucite candy dish with the lift-up top inscribed, "Have a nosh with Arlene and Jerry."

On Saturday nights, when my parents hosted dinner parties, my role changed from Dad's barmaid to Mom's assistant chef. Our quiet kitchen would erupt into a cacophony of clattering trays, clanking ice cubes, and Mom's signature three-inch heels clicking against the linoleum floor as she scurried around the kitchen, readying dinner for our impending company.

In the kitchen it was just the two of us, side by side at the countertop, working under bright light thrown from a beaded chandelier, a dozen giant white mushrooms looming before us. One by one, we gently wiped the fleshy fungus, each one larger than my eight-year-old fist. "They're a lot of work but they look impressive," she said. The supersize mushrooms had been purchased especially for the occasion at the California Mushroom Farm in nearby Santa Fe Springs, where, hand in hand, my mother and I walked through the cool, dark warehouse, my T-shirt pulled over my nose to buffer the overwhelming stench of horse manure.

Homemade stuffed mushrooms, fried wontons, and spinach triangles wrapped in phyllo dough weren't the only reason I delighted in my parents' entertainment. The chiming of the front doorbell thrilled me. Guests arrived through the elegant foyer, where, at night, a crystal chandelier illuminated wall-to-wall travertine floor and wall tiles. The house came alive with chatter and laughter.

My mother, frosted hair teased high in a bouffant, double-strand white pearls on her neck, and bright coral red on her lips, greeted guests with a cheek-to-cheek air kiss. My father collected coats and stoles, and Mom led guests into the shag-carpeted family room, where the men, wearing leisure suits with wide-collared shirts, hunched on low stools around the coffee table and swigged Harvey Wallbanger highballs. The women, wearing wrap dresses and platform shoes, sat with their legs crossed on the sectional sofa and sipped chardonnay from Waterford glasses.

Following drinks and hors d'oeuvres, guests moved into the dining room. There, with my bedtime approaching, I fluttered from guest to guest, refilling glasses from a water pitcher and breathing in the exotic scent of perfume and aftershave, watching the adults drink and flirt. It was all so glamorous.

"Look at mother's little helper!" Beverly would say as I filled her glass. Her husband, Sammy, my dad's best friend and our family doctor, would give one of my curly pigtails a playful tug, and Beverly would turn to my mother. "Arlene, she is a little doll."

"She is," my mom would say. "I think we'll keep her."

• ———— •

Even though I was regularly in their presence, I longed for a closeness with my parents that felt beyond my reach. I often lay for hours across the bedspread on their king-size bed in the shadows cast by a towering eucalyptus tree outside the window while my mother leaned back in her cane-back chair, her feet propped on her desk, and chatted on the phone with friends. Sometimes I wandered off the bed over to the desk cabinet, took out the S&H Green Stamps catalog, and browsed through the toy section, circling all the things I wanted. After what seemed an interminable amount of time, I'd tap my mother's shoulder. "Mom?"

I knew I shouldn't interrupt her, but she was so close I couldn't help myself. Despite her always saying no, she didn't like games, I hoped that this once she might sit on the floor with me and play Barbies or Monopoly or run through the house and play hide-and-seek—I hoped that this once, she would set aside time just for me.

"Hold on, Phyllis," she'd say, cupping the receiver. "What is it, honey?"

"When are you going to be off the phone?"

"I don't know, sweetie. Why don't you go play?"

I never bothered concealing my disappointment, because she'd already have the receiver back to her ear. "Where were we, Phyllis?"

Eventually, I'd get tired of waiting and retreat to my bedroom, where I looked out through the slatted wood blinds into the empty street.

Some mornings, I'd go into my parents' master bathroom and watch my mother sitting at her custom-built vanity on a leopard-upholstered stool (the only seat in the house low enough for her to firmly plant her feet on the floor) and putting the finishing touches on her makeup: a single squeeze of the eyelash curler to the naturally long lashes of each eye; a smooth swipe of L'Oréal "pink shell" over her full lips, softly frosting the coral undercoat; and a final application of hairspray to her carefully teased hair. This last step always prompted the same singsongy warning: "Step away from the spray"—my cue to move back into her bedroom. There, from a safe distance, I would watch my mom shake a can of Aqua Net and spray with wild abandon, sending into the air a thick chemical fog.

I delighted in playing with her makeup; the blueprint of her cosmetics is still mapped out in my mind as vividly as is the layout of our house. The drawer on the right held mascara, blush, and eye shadow in varying shades of blue—the drawer on the left, a stack of false eyelashes and adhesive glue. My favorite item was the retractable lipstick brush. It was the size of a tube of lipstick, but more slender and tapered at both ends. It was sage green and had a plastic button on one end that, when pressed, sent a brush out the opposite end. The tiny brush allowed my mom to apply color to her lips with the precision of a diamond cutter. Each push of the little button also brought a satisfying click—a sound as reliable as Mrs. Obermeyer's doorbell.

On occasion, I would wander over to my dad's side of the bathroom and peek into his sparsely filled medicine cabinet: Arrid deodorant cream in a jar, electric razor, and first-aid ointments, reminders of his easy good sense. I loved to explore the nooks and crannies in my parents' bathroom, sliding open the long and narrow medicine cabinet, flipping up the protective brass hood of the recessed toilet paper holder, and taking *National Geographic* issues from the built-in magazine rack and staring at the exotic covers. It wasn't a fancy room—the floor was linoleum and the counters laminate—but the comfort I found there gave order to my world.

And then, one morning, that sense of order vanished. It was an unusually cloudy day, and low light filtered through the row of frosted privacy glass windows situated high above the built-in cabinets, casting a dull gloom over the long, narrow bathroom. The quiet shuffling of my mother's makeup applicators was punctuated by the frustrated barks of Hilda, the gray Weimaraner next door—a dog who was frequently set off by an array of backyard fauna: skittish crows, foraging coyotes, and, on occasion, our provoking outdoor cat, Whiskers.

I stood behind my mother and stared at her reflection in the freestanding backlit makeup mirror, observing an older version of my own oval face and big blue eyes. "What's this for?" I held up a black tube and removed the lid to reveal a creamy beige stick.

"That's to conceal the bags under your eyes. You won't need that for a long time."

"And this?" I unscrewed a bottle of beige liquid.

"Careful, that's expensive. It's foundation. It helps smooth out my complexion and hide the wrinkles." She turned away from the mirror and wagged a finger at me, and the ruffled sleeve of her long peach satin nightgown slid away from her wrist, revealing a nickel-size curling iron burn mark. "Always take good care of your skin. Your face will thank you later."

She rose and I followed her like a puppy into her bedroom, careful not to step on the billowy robe that flowed behind her like the train of a royal wedding gown. As she dressed I walked over to her bureau, slid open her jewelry drawer, and picked up a long strand of pearls. I loved how the pearls felt as they spilled into my hands. I wanted to try them on.

"I might be late to pick you up from school today. I have to take your brother to tennis finals."

The room fell silent. I didn't hear her explanation about why Adam's match might run late, or the sound of Hilda's relentless woofing and growling, or the frenetic pulse of my heartbeat, which thumped wildly in my ears. I suddenly felt off balance, as though I had crossed into another dimension; I stared at my mother through a blur of tears as she sat at the edge of her bed, a knee bent to her chest, slipping a nylon stocking over her toes.

"How late?" I managed to croak. But my only thought was, *What if she never comes back?*

•———•

Within weeks of that incident, even the briefest of separations became excruciating. I shadowed my mom around the house and refused to play with my best friend, Cassy, across the street. When she used the bathroom, I waited outside the door until she came out. Any time she left the room, I asked her where she was going. I skipped any activity that separated me from my mother for too long.

Adam stood in my bedroom one afternoon, thick tufts of dark hair peaking from beneath his white tennis cap. "Why do you always want to be with Mom?" he demanded. "Why don't you go anywhere or do anything without her?"

His questions humiliated me. But what could I say? I didn't know why. I didn't know what a trauma was, or that I'd suffered one when I'd gotten lost on the beach in Florida. I didn't know that when something triggers a reminder of the trauma, the intense fear returns. I didn't know that I would carry my childhood anxiety with me into adulthood and that I might never fully bounce back from Boca.

•———•

My stomach began to churn the moment our car rolled out of the garage. "Please, Mom," I pleaded as she drove me toward Hebrew school. "I don't want to go!"

"We talked about this, honey. You can't just stay home all the time," she said, her voice characteristically calm and matter-of-fact.

I knew she was right. At eight years old, I was old enough to understand that my behavior wasn't normal. But fear overrode my shame and embarrassment.

"But Adam doesn't have to go!" I protested.

"Janie, I told you, your brother has regionals today."

I could see in my mother's eyes in the rearview mirror that I was getting nowhere. A wave of desperation flooded through me. I tried a different tactic. "If I go, will you stay?"

"Honey, I'm sorry," she said, pulling into Robbie Sherman's driveway, impatience rising in her voice. "I can't wait around for two hours. I have to drive Adam to his match."

I wanted to cry, but Robbie's freckled face appeared in the window, obliging me to pull myself together. I slid over to make room in the backseat, pressed my forehead against the window, and stared off in the distance. My throat burned with sadness.

The twenty-minute car ride felt eternal. At the top of the hill, a square building draped in pale and tawny Jerusalem stone loomed. My mom pulled up in the drop-off lane, and I gave her one last pleading look. As soon as I closed the car door, the station wagon pulled away. I watched it make its way down the hill until its red taillights faded into blurry specks.

In the classroom, we sat listening to Ms. Hersh's lesson about charity. She held up a colorful box covered with Hebrew words I couldn't read, giving it a few quick shakes. "Who brought change from home for our *tzedakah* box today?" she asked.

Normally I wouldn't have hesitated to drop in coins, rewarded by that delicate clinking sound, but today the word "home" prompted tears to stream down my face, tears that only fell faster when I saw the other kids watching me cry. How could I consider giving when all I could think of was how I needed my mother, how desperate I was to be home?

When I refused to go back the following week, my parents formed a plan that would help me tolerate religious school without tears—and, as it would turn out, without dignity. My grandma was recruited to attend with me.

For years, my grandma had volunteered at my public school library repairing books. She sat at a wooden desk, hunched attentively over the books, cutting, taping, and mending damaged spines. With patience and precision, she breathed new life into old books. I was accustomed to her helping out at school, and I even enjoyed her presence. The other kids did too. "Hi, Mrs. Schaffer!" they greeted her. She would look up from a broken book, pale hazel eyes smiling behind her bifocals, and respond, "Hello, hello," always a double nod, and then she returned to her work.

At religious school, however, I resented her call to service and was ashamed that it was me, not a book, that was in disrepair.

CHAPTER 10: DON'T TOUCH MY MOUSTACHE

Tokyo – August 2001

Walking through the busy terminal, everything felt foreign, from the sterile, modern architecture to the signs written in vertical characters. We'd just landed and I already felt lost in translation.

We got into a taxi waiting at the curb. I was surprised when I reached for the passenger door and it swung open by itself; no one had told me that cab doors in Japan opened and closed automatically.

That wasn't the only difference between this cab and the city cabs I knew. The taxi was spotless, lace doilies covered the seats, and a courteous driver sporting white gloves greeted us in Japanese.

"What did he say?" I asked Wim, who had warned me, before we'd gotten in, that cab drivers in Japan didn't speak English.

"He asked, 'Did you learn fluent Japanese on the twelve-hour flight?'" Wim joked.

We quickly learned that the language barrier wasn't our only problem. Japan has a very different address system than the West. Streets in Japan don't have names, and blocks are numbered in order of the buildings' ages.

"New Otani," Wim instructed the driver.

The driver spewed back exaggerated-sounding Japanese words. After several minutes of futile exchange, we handed the driver a map and pointed to our hotel. Finally, he nodded, and off we went.

• —— •

For the next week, we surveyed dozens of four-bedroom apartments. One afternoon, we stood inside a unit at the Grand Tower Residence. I glanced around the room, which was accented with Asian accessories, and was reminded of a decorative fan that had once adorned the wall of our Rosemead apartment. If I had found it challenging making that place our own, what would it be like here?

"It feels spacious," I said to Yui, our real estate agent. And by Tokyo standards, where most people live in apartments the size of college dorm rooms, it was. But I knew at first glance—observing the white living room walls and bland, soulless architecture—that I could never feel at home there.

We had barely crossed the *genkan*, the entrance area where shoes are taken off, when I felt an urge that couldn't be ignored. I turned to Yui. "Excuse me, I'm going to need a private room that has an electrical outlet. One that will work with an American appliance."

She led me to one of the bedrooms. I closed the door behind me, lifted a heavy black satchel off my shoulder, and sat on the floor against the wall.

My breasts were hard and swollen. I assembled the device, plugged in, and set the breast pump on the highest suction. I felt immediate relief as the machine siphoned out a day's worth of milk from my breast—milk that was intended for my six-month-old daughter, which I would instead pump and dump. The breast pump whirred loudly in a syncopated, loud-to-soft rhythm. My body relaxed, but my mind wouldn't. Nursing a plastic siphon while my daughter drank from a plastic bottle magnified the distance between us and exacerbated the misery of being so far from my children. As for my own parents, we already lived 3,000 miles away from them. Now I was considering stretching it 2,000 more. I played the same questions over and over in my mind: *Can I really do this? Start fresh with a new home and new friends? Learn a language composed of characters? Master the metric system?*

"How are you doing in there?" Wim yelled through the door.

"One down, one to go," I yelled back over the whirring of the pump. I glanced around the bedroom of the current renters— fellow Americans, I figured, based on the box of Cap'n Crunch I had noticed on the kitchen counter. I searched the room for clues to expat life. Before me was a blend of old and new: a modern platform bed atop an Oriental rug, no doubt a souvenir from a side trip. Did they send their kids to the American school we had interviewed? Did they belong to the American Club we had visited? Had making the decision to move here been as agonizing for them as it felt to Wim and me?

Even the idea of taking an elevator up and down each day to our "home" made my stomach drop. I had associated Tokyo living with backyard cherry blossoms and manicured gardens, not high-rise apartments and concrete terraces. The simple ride up to the Grand Tower Residence apartment had felt uncomfortable, and not just because the three of us—Wim, Yui, and I—had been compressed in a closet-size elevator.

I had noticed a missing number on the panel and asked Yui, "Why is there no fourth floor?"

"In Japan, the number four is considered unlucky, so the elevator is not marked for the fourth floor," she answered in her impeccable English. "In Japanese, the word for four can be pronounced 'shi,' which means death. Giving someone four gifts is like saying, 'I hope you die.'"

I considered the four in my address, the two fours in my middle child's birthday, and the three fours in our phone number and pondered my expat fate.

•———•

Yui's words continued to reverberate in my mind that night as we lay on the hard mattress in our hotel room discussing our prospects, something we had done nearly every night since Wim had been offered a job in Tokyo four months earlier. Should we move? Shouldn't we move? So much seemed at stake. Our happiness. Our welfare. Our sanity.

I exhaled loudly. "Remind me why we want to move here?"

"Money. Culture. Adventure. Geisha girls?"

"Seriously, Wim. Say we really move here. When are we going to see our families? I can't imagine your parents traveling to Asia to visit us. Your mother can't even drive over the George Washington Bridge to visit us in Rye. I'm not even sure my folks would visit, and they're thousands of miles closer. And what about my grandma Rose and Gram? We don't see them enough as it is."

"I've heard that a lot of people summer in the States because it gets so hot and humid here, so we'd see our family then."

"Only once a year?" I groaned.

"This job would probably only be for three years."

"But what if it went longer?"

I fidgeted under the covers as I thought about what two American couples had told us at dinner several nights before: how the first three years were the hardest, but once you got over the hump, it was tempting to stay longer. One couple had been living in Tokyo for five years, the other for seven.

"My salary will almost double and my company will cover our rent. And you can have your own cook, driver, full-time help—everything."

"Can I get that without moving to Tokyo?" I was only half joking.

"If we lived here we could travel to other countries on holiday breaks. China. Thailand. Singapore. Everything is so close."

"I know. But the kids are still so young."

"There's never going to be a perfect time, Janie. I only have one chance at this."

The life he described sounded so good. But why did it have to be here?

•———•

The warm, peaceful environment of the hotel spa embraced us the moment we walked in the door, eager to vanquish the stress of last night's conversation. The clerk greeted us with a bow and led us down a hallway of doors to our individual rooms. As I entered the dimly lit massage room, I took it all in—water trickling from a small corner fountain, the soft glow of votive candles perched on a bamboo accent table, the large, gold Buddha staring down at me from its high perch on a pedestal. I disrobed, stretched myself facedown on the padded massage table, and covered my naked body with a soft sheet. I heard a gentle knock at the door and, craning my neck, saw a petite young woman dressed in a crisp white uniform enter.

She bowed once she was in the room. Without speaking, she lathered her hands with massage oil. It smelled leafy and lemony.

She rested her warm hands on my back and I immediately felt yesterday's tension melt away. The floor creaked under her feet as she glided her hands across my skin. She kneaded her knuckles into my flesh like it was putty, working it with strong, deep strokes. I thought of Wim and hoped he was relaxed and enjoying this as much as I was.

I sank into a light doze but was soon awakened by her movements, which had suddenly become too strong and too deep. I considered speaking up, but I was afraid I'd offend her. After a few more minutes, I cared less about her feelings and more about my pain.

"Excuse me, can you please massage more gently?" I asked. "Thank you."

She paused and in a shrill voice shrieked, "Don't touch my mustache!"

I raised my head but saw not a trace of hair growth on her flawless complexion. I sank back down and tried to focus on the soft music, but it was challenging, what with the heels of her palms digging deeper and deeper into the bony structure that was my spine. Her steely strength seemed incompatible with her five-foot frame. I felt less like I was getting a massage and more like I was having my bones reset.

"Gentler, please," I urged. "Thank you."

She paused again. "Don't touch my mustache!" Then she began pounding me like a side of beef, karate chopping my back with the force and fury of a samurai warrior, until she had rearranged every one of my internal organs.

At last, she stopped and bowed.

I raised my head weakly and squeaked, "Thank you."

"Don't touch my mustache!" she squawked, then quietly

exited the room. In her dainty hands she held a small object that was likely a crumpled towel but which I suspected was my spleen.

I lay in solitude, wallowing in my newfound pain. Finally, I mustered the will to rise and got dressed. I stumbled back to the lobby, feeling altogether broken.

Wim, sipping a tall glass of cucumber water, looked energized and refreshed. He took in my crumpled face. "You look like you were just stampeded by a herd of elephants."

I shook my head and frowned. "Don't touch my mustache."

"What?"

"That's what the masseuse said when I asked her to be gentle!"

"Don't touch my mustache?"

"Something like that. 'Don't tashi mashie,'" I mimicked in a high voice.

"*Do itashimashite?*" Wim snorted with laugher. "That means 'you're welcome.'"

•———•

That night, under the crisp bedsheets of the New Otani, thoughts of my massage taunted me like a cruel metaphor. A move to Japan might be wonderful in theory but painful in reality. I feared that the massage represented just one of many future instances of misunderstanding.

After brushing his hair (a nighttime ritual I'd never understood), Wim climbed in beside me.

"I feel like I'm already caught between two cultures and we haven't even moved yet," I said. "I want to support your career. I just don't want the journey to destroy our marriage and our family."

He reminded me that we'd always enjoyed learning about different cultures and traveling. "We met when we were backpacking through Spain!" he said.

How could I impress upon him how scared I was to move so far from home, especially with three young children to take care of?

He fluffed his feather pillow and turned over. "Let's talk about this tomorrow." He kissed me good night and turned off the bedside lamp.

•———•

I was dreaming that my kids had taken the wrong bus to their new school and had ended up lost and wandering through unnamed streets when the phone startled us awake with piercing, high-pitched double rings that would have sounded unwelcoming at any hour.

Wim flicked the light on and picked up the receiver. "Hello?"

For a moment I couldn't remember where I was or what bed I was in. I sat up and squinted into the bright light. The tightness of my swollen breasts told me that at least several hours had passed. The red lines on the clock indicated 2:44 a.m.

He shook his head. "Mom, do you know what time it is here?" After several minutes he cupped the receiver and whispered, "She's really upset. It's 105 degrees there, and she and my dad have been cooped up with the kids."

I listened for a few more minutes, and then I slipped out of bed to use the bathroom. The marble tile chilled my bare feet as I stood before the mirror and unbuttoned my red silk pajama top. I reached into my bra, pulled out two circular nursing pads, warm and soggy with baby milk, and replaced them with two fresh pads, gently easing them over the painful mounds of hot marbles that were my breasts.

When I climbed back into bed, Wim was still on the phone, trying to offer his mother what comfort he could from 6,000 miles away. "No, Mom," he said patiently, "we haven't made a decision yet."

That explained her outburst. Of course she was anxious about this move too. I'd been so concerned about how my family and I would adapt that I hadn't stopped to think about the effect it would have on our extended families—missing birthday celebrations and bar mitzvahs, holidays and hockey games. Wim's mother had literally just given me a wakeup call.

Wim hung up the phone. He looked shaken. "I've never heard her that upset before," he said. Then he switched off the light and flipped onto his side.

"Wim?"

"Yeah."

"I don't want to do it." My voice cracked and tears spilled from my eyes. "Three years feels like too many to be so far away."

"Are you crying?"

I nodded in the dark.

He reached over and wiped my tears with the edge of the comforter. "This decision has to be mutual. The move doesn't just affect me; it affects our whole family. I can't do this without you being on board."

I rolled toward him and laid my hand on his chest, taking comfort in his warm body and familiar scent.

He heaved a deep sigh and placed his hand on mine.

"I'm sorry," I said, feeling like I was stepping on his dreams.

He clasped my fingers, and we fell asleep.

CHAPTER 11: WE WANT IT ALL

Raymond Ave, Rye – August 2006

I was on a mission. We'd hired Luke just two weeks earlier and already I'd become a regular at the Construction and Home Repair aisle at Barnes & Noble. For hours I'd sit on the floor with piles of books stacked beside me, taking fastidious notes on all things renovation.

Luke had asked us to create what he called a "program" that included everything we wanted in a house. I'd always fantasized about owning my dream home, but much like the sex dream where the mystery lover is faceless, I'd never had a specific image in my mind.

"Do we create our dream list first and see if it fits the budget, or do we determine what we can afford and then decide what goes in it?" I asked Wim, almost giddy.

"Luke said to start with the program," Wim said.

We knew how much a house would cost per square foot to remodel. We figured we could get a ballpark estimate on spending and then work backward, reducing space and fantasy features until we had a home that matched our budget. Wim would ensure that we didn't stick ourselves with a house that we someday couldn't get rid of because it was too costly for its own good.

But for now, on paper, we could have it all without worrying about money.

I'd always wanted a house with a front porch, where I envisioned us sitting in wicker chairs, sipping lemonade, and waving to the neighbors.

"What about a stone accent on the outside?" Wim said.

"Wouldn't it be nice to have a fireplace in the bedroom?" I responded.

And so it went. We created a growing list of features—shingle vs. aluminum, skylights vs. no skylights, exposed rafters vs. smooth ceilings, until we'd covered every square inch of our new house.

•————•

The next time we met, we presented Luke with the document. As we sat with him in our small breakfast nook and listened to the sound of water running in the toilet a few feet away, I wondered how many times over the years we had debated whether to expand the kitchen and relocate the oddly placed downstairs bathroom. But I had the new house to obsess over now.

"Rules and instructions," he read aloud. "We want the house to feel spacious yet cozy, a home that has the quality and character of an old house but has modern amenities." He flipped the page. "Energy efficiency: Consider plumbing in one general area to reduce pipe distance and conserve energy. Interior Design: Make sure the doorways, hallways, and stairways are wide enough to move furniture through."

The list went on and on.

In just two weeks, our program had grown from a rough outline to a ten-page, single-spaced, typewritten document. We began with general concepts, such as, "This is our forever home, so let's do it right," and then proceeded to include everything there was to know about home building, from verbiage on the best way to install hydronic radiant heat throughout the house to how to determine adequate turnaround radius in a driveway. It was a cross between a fairy tale wish list and a *Home Remodeling for Dummies* manual. We'd included so much detail and instruction, it was if we were planning to design the house ourselves.

"We're only going to get one shot at this," Wim had said. Still, as Luke sat at our kitchen table looking over our myriad needs, I couldn't help but wonder what was going through his head.

Coming up with the criteria had been challenging since, as amateurs, we didn't know much about home remodeling and didn't yet speak the language. "We want one of those faucets that comes out of the wall over the stove to fill the pot," we'd written, and, "Make sure those strips of wood around the windows are simple." It was like being asked to interpret Dostoevsky without ever having learned to read. Eventually, I would learn vocabulary like "pot filler" and "casings," and I'd even use them in complete sentences.

"You did your homework," Luke said finally.

I felt proud, thinking about all the hours of research we'd done.

Above Wim's head hung a series of four decorative plates, two on each side of a mirror designed to look like a window with open shutters. The first plate had a drawing of a red apple; the last plate was just seeds; and the plates in between showed a bitten apple and a core. Wim and I had often pondered whether the series started with the seeds or with the whole apple, much in the same way we had asked ourselves if we should start with what we wanted or what we could afford. We didn't know at the time that it doesn't matter which came first, the apple or the seeds—it's all about whether you've bitten off more than you can chew.

·———·

"This is just a starting point," Luke said a few weeks later as he unraveled a set of plans across the kitchen table. It was early, and fall light streamed in through the small kitchen window; the day was filled with promise.

I told him about a book I'd come across recently—*The Not So Big House* by Susan Susanka. "She talks about designing rooms to feel interconnected and intimate," I said. "Luxury that comes from detail rather than spaciousness. Quality over quantity." Reading Susanka's book had been like a revelation for both Wim and me. We had now taken her philosophy on as our personal paradigm—a way to frame exactly the type of aesthetic we were after, one we hadn't been able to articulate before.

"I'll add that to the program." Luke smiled and made a note in his book. "So, here's your foyer," he said, pressing down the edges of his drawing so it lay flat. I looked down at the plans and froze. Wim looked crestfallen as well; I knew we were thinking the same thing. The drawing depicted a massive round entryway that looked more like a grand ballroom than a foyer—the exact opposite of what we now wanted. There was a double winding staircase leading up to the second floor. I didn't know what I had expected, but it wasn't this.

"You wanted a house that's unique, that doesn't have the same features as every other house," Luke began his pitch. "So, I thought of a circular foyer. It's something you don't see every day. The idea just kind of came to me!" He looked up and his voice dropped. "You don't like it."

"Well." Wim looked from me to the drawing. "I don't feel like it's the look we're going for."

Luke's face fell.

"It's beautiful. Don't get me wrong," Wim said. "Maybe . . ."

If we were the Trapp Family Singers, I wanted to say. I pictured a scene from *The Sound of Music,* only it was our three children wearing lederhosen and standing in height order on the staircase, belting out "Edelweiss."

"No need to apologize," he said, running a perfectly trimmed thumbnail repeatedly across a small crease at the edge of the drawing, as if rubbing it would eliminate the damage. "It's my job to get it right."

•———•

"Look at this," Wim said, moments after we'd shown Luke to the door. "That's not a foyer. That's the lobby at the Ritz-Carlton."

I laughed, though I could have easily been crying.

"Seriously, Janie. We just gave this guy a ton of money. I'm pissed." I could see the vein at his temple pulsing.

"Me too," I said. My God, what had we done? A double staircase was the last thing we'd wanted. We'd already given Luke the equivalent of a year's college tuition to draw up these plans, and he clearly didn't get us at all. We'd been so diligent about picking the perfect person to create the perfect house. We'd asked for "cozy," and we'd gotten nouveau riche. What had happened?

This wasn't entirely Luke's fault, I reminded Wim. We'd experienced our *Not So Big House* revelation after we'd given him our program.

I sighed. "What's going to happen? We just hired the guy. We can't fire him."

"He's going back to the drawing board," Wim said. He was still shaking his head as he walked away.

•———•

Wim leaned over his own drawings at the dining room table one Sunday morning in November. He was wearing old flannel pajama bottoms festooned with reindeers. His socks, the same wool pair he'd worn in Switzerland, were so riddled with holes I could see his baby toe poking through. Watching him from the doorway, I made a mental note to buy him new ones, though the likelihood was it probably wouldn't get done. Everything had fallen by the wayside since we'd started this project.

Wim took a swig of coffee from a mug that our friends Ron and Nina had given him for his birthday the previous week, the words "40TH BIRTHDAY!" emblazoned in gold on the side. The other side said, "CELEBRATE!" though we barely had. At the time, nothing seemed more important than designing our house.

Snow was falling on the wood deck behind Wim, sticking to the rhododendrons, which had begun to sag from the extra weight, much in the same way I felt Wim and I had begun to sink under the weight of our house plans. In some ways, it felt good to me to be making decisions, feeling a sense of camaraderie, having a sense of purpose. But for months we'd been running in circles, unable to find a floor plan that we were happy with.

Not only that. We also hadn't understood that there were things we couldn't change even if we wanted to—stairway and load-bearing wall locations, low ceilings—either because it was too costly or because doing so compromised the structural integrity of the house.

To further complicate matters, as much as I wanted our house to be a reflection of our family, I found myself suddenly thinking about my childhood home and holding up a California ranch, with its open floor plan for easy entertaining, as my ideal. I conjured up warm memories of holiday dinners spent in the formal dining room, my grandma ladling out steaming bowls of matzo ball soup. After dinner, we kids would move into the adjacent living room to play pool while the adults remained at the table, schmoozing and sipping coffee.

I wanted to create a version of that with Wim in our new home. I craved a floor plan of intimately connected rooms, even though that configuration was totally inconsistent with the center-hall colonial we were working with. This, I suppose, is how we found ourselves in possession of a house plan with a living room and dining room that didn't flow with the rest of the house, and a foyer the size of a supermarket.

Pinpointing what we wanted in a home had grown into a complicated exercise in examining how we lived compared to how we wanted to live; what we wanted to keep the same versus what we wanted to change. We asked ourselves, which rooms do we spend most of our time in, and why?

It seemed logical to me that our home office, where I'd recently started spending time writing, should be a short stroll from the kitchen and the coffee maker, and only a slightly longer stroll to the garage where I parked my minivan. "I want my work area to be in the center of things," I told Wim. As I said it, I realized that, despite all the volunteering I'd done at my children's schools and at our synagogue, it had been a long time since I'd strung the words "I" and "work" together in one sentence. My new daily ritual—rising at 5:00 a.m. and jumping out of bed to transpose my thoughts to page—felt important, productive, and satisfying, even if I wasn't getting paid to do it. For the first time in years, I felt a kind of ecstatic joy in being so engaged with something that I didn't even notice if I was hungry or tired.

But Wim said, "You can't put rooms wherever you want." I knew he was right, that we had to stay within the house's footprint, but I didn't want to accept it. We'd been so particular about finding the right house, and now here we were, working around someone else's floor plans.

The one thing we did agree on was creating a guestroom for my parents to stay in when they visited from California. Our current home had no guestroom, so my parents always had to stay in hotels. It was expensive and inconvenient and made us feel like inadequate hosts. Wim and I wanted to accommodate them with a comfortable bedroom and an attached full bath on the first floor.

We were also thinking ahead and planning to "age in place," the new term we'd learned for planning a design that takes into account a couple's changing needs with age. Wide doorways, levers instead of doorknobs, light switches at a lower, wheelchair-accessible height.

"The day might come when we're too old and creaky to climb the stairs," I told Wim.

"With a first-floor master suite, the office suite can become our own built-in ambulatory service center," Wim said, laughing. But it was no joke. Over the fourteen years we'd been married, a lot had changed; our personalities, our bodies, even our sex life had waxed and waned. The further we got into planning, the more we both realized that, as much as anything, this house was a step toward making our marriage more permanent—a commitment to aging *together*. That even if marriage hadn't turned out to be the Cinderella story I'd grown up believing it to be, that didn't mean I couldn't try for the fairy-tale ending.

•———•

Even after reducing the size of our foyer by half, with an office and a guestroom both situated on the first floor, our "not so big" house was beginning to bulge.

"We've run out of floor area on the first floor," Luke said one rainy winter afternoon.

"What?" I said, not believing what I was hearing. The rain was falling loud and hard on the roof, and I thought that I'd misheard him.

"If we want to keep everything else we designed in the program, you'll have to settle for a one-car garage," he said after providing a mind-numbing explanation of our town's policy.

He might as well have told me I'd have to live in a yurt.

"A two-car garage is one of the top features on our list," I said. I refrained from adding, "And I didn't move from California to New York to spend my cold winters scraping snow off my windshield," because I didn't want Luke to silently brand the word "princess" before my name.

"Maybe we should consider putting the guest suite in the basement," Wim said.

I pulled a face. "The dungeon?" I pictured the dark, dank space under the first floor. "Why not just leave my parents out to die in the snow like the Eskimos?"

"That would solve the problem," Luke said. "I don't mean if you left your parents out in the snow," he added.

"There's a lot of space in the basement," Wim said.

I thought about the spacious, sunny, above-ground space my parents had provided for us when Wim and I had lived with them before we married. Finally, we had the opportunity to reciprocate. "The ceilings are low," I said. "You know my mom has claustrophobia. She'd never survive down there."

Luke cleared his throat and looked away. "Why don't you two discuss it and we can meet again soon?"

As we rose from the table, I found myself comparing Luke and Wim. Luke was taller, Wim broader in the shoulders. I wondered, *If Luke were making this decision with his wife, what would they decide?*

The following week, Wim stood bent over his drawings, completely absorbed, oblivious to his exposed toe and to the snow cascading over the backyard. He looked weary as he furiously erased a doorway he'd just drawn. For the past week we'd spent endless hours online, studying floor plans to help us define the space, but still, I was surprised to find him there, pencil in hand, taking a crack at the plans himself. I wanted to reassure him that we'd eventually come up with a floor plan that worked, but even I was beginning to have doubts.

"Where'd you get the drafting paper?" I pointed to a roll of vellum, a thin and translucent type of paper used for tracing over architectural plans. Its smooth, delicate quality reminded me of a cross between the tissue paper I used for stuffing gift bags and the waxed paper my grandmother used to lovingly line the glass jar lids of her homemade garlicky dill pickles with.

"I borrowed it from Luke," he said without looking up.

"Isn't this his job?"

Words tumbled from Wim faster than the snow falling from the sky.

"We expected a six-month renovation. We're already six months into this, and we don't have any drawings to show for it. Drawings we've already paid for. Paid a lot for." His face looked so tense his eyeballs were practically shaking in their sockets.

"We can't blame Luke," I said, trying to calm him. "We're the ones who keep changing the plans and changing our minds about what we want."

It was true: Wim and I would stay up late, letting our minds go wild with ideas about what our dream home would look like. Then, the next day, we would start over again with a completely different idea.

"Janie, we own two houses," he yelled. "We are paying two mortgages and property taxes times two. Time is ticking. It's do or die."

• —— •

One morning, as I was sitting at the dining room table studying house plans, Wim glanced over my shoulder and pointed to a circular mark in a corner of the family room. "What's that?" he asked.

"A tree," I said.

"Why is there a tree on the blueprints?"

"I asked Luke to draw it in. I wanted to make sure that our ficus would fit the space if we end up having to reduce the size of the office."

I cherished our ficus. We'd hauled that tree all the way from California to New York; I couldn't abandon it now.

Wim stared at me in disbelief. "You actually had him create another set of plans just to show a house plant?"

"Yeah, why?" I asked.

"Janie, we have to pay for those plans."

My eyes widened. "We do?"

"Of course! He charges us every time he prints a new set!" he said.

"Well I didn't know," I said, feeling foolish.

Wim made no effort to mask his annoyance. But who could blame him? I was at the mercy of my ever-present, stress-related, obsessive-compulsive focus on minutiae.

Still, I longed for an *I Love Lucy* happy ending, with me expressing chagrin, Wim forgiving me, and the two of us embracing, encircled by a satin heart. Instead, our bickering was escalating to the point that I'd begun to wonder if by the end of this project, like Lucy and Ricky, we would need separate beds. Or worse, separate houses.

Hunched over the plans like a rabbi among the Dead Sea Scrolls, we often studied until the wee hours of the morning, reworking Luke's drawings over and over. But by the end of the month, we realized we would have to make compromises.

"Let's bump my parents to the basement," I said one evening.

"Really?" Wim said.

I shrugged. "It's more important to have an office we'll use every day than to have a first-floor guest suite that gets used twice a year."

He nodded and started throwing out ideas: The office could double as a guestroom. We could even build in extra closet space.

"Maybe instead of a half bath next to the office, we could build a full bath," I said.

And our dreaming began all over again.

Eventually, we settled on a guestroom location that felt good to us, and we bid out the remodel to several builders. We'd expected some bids to be high, but after a long month of waiting, the three proposals that came in were more expensive than we ever could have imagined.

"I just don't know." Wim closed his eyes and rubbed his hand down the side of his face. We were sitting at the computer, looking at a spreadsheet he had created to help compare the bids.

"They're even higher than Luke expected," I said in dismay.

"I feel like I want to throw up," Wim said. "After all the money we paid for this house, the idea of spending this amount just to make it livable . . ."

"And still not get everything we want." I got up and poured us both another cup of coffee, stirring just the right amount of cream into his. It was coffee I'd brewed in the same French press Wim had had in Switzerland, a classic-looking glass jar with a beautiful stainless steel frame that made the perfect amount of coffee for two people. Wim and I both cherished our morning ritual of boiling water, pouring it over the coffee grounds, waiting six minutes for them to seep, and then, finally, lowering the plunger with a satisfying push slow and steady. There was something about the effort involved that made the coffee taste even better.

"I had an idea about the basement guestroom," I said. "What if we build taller windows to let in more light?"

Wim gave me a look that said, *You've got to be kidding.* A familiar look that sometimes made me not want to open my mouth. "You can't just build taller windows," he said.

"Why not?"

"Because we have to work with the existing ceiling height."

I closed my eyes, embarrassed for saying my idea out loud.

"Unless . . ." He stared off.

"Unless what?" I asked, hoping he hadn't grown so discouraged that he wanted to cut our losses and scrap the project altogether. But what he said next shocked me.

"We tear down the house."

CHAPTER 12: PEEING AT VERSAILLES

Rosemead, CA – November 1992

Our Rosemead apartment faced a grassy, tree-lined court-yard adjacent to a gated swimming pool that, as full-time students, we rarely used. Inside our six-hundred-square-foot two-bedroom, one-bath unit, beige drapes hung like protective coveralls over beige walls, and commercial brown wall-to-wall carpet covered the floors. In the family room, the carpet had faded at the edges to a distinctive swimmer's-hair green from exposure to the bright sun that filtered through the patio sliding door. The few pieces of furniture that we owned—a mishmash of second-hand items—took up most of the small room.

Along one wall sat a sofa we had purchased at a tent sale; along an adjacent wall, a mauve futon I had inherited from a college roommate. Completing the sitting area was a large oak coffee table, matching end table, coordinating side lamp, and antique replica quail paperweight-and-candlesnuffer set my mom had purchased for my dad's legal office and passed on to Wim and me when my dad retired.

Shortly after his retirement we sat with my parents around their kitchen table discussing the economy—mostly, listening to my dad's views on wealth. "The economy may be showing signs of improvement, but the climate could change," Dad told us. "There's the possibility that Clinton's health care reform, if it happens, will add costs to businesses and stifle the creation of new jobs. Your graduate degrees will be more important than ever." He removed his silver-rimmed glasses and rubbed his eyes.

"Jerry, they haven't even graduated yet," my mother said. "Let them finish school first."

Dad blinked twice and returned the glasses to his face. The stems slid through his short gray hair, which, though it was receding at the temples, was still fairly thick. "I'm fortunate to be able to retire at fifty-eight, when most people are still working."

"Now that he's retired, he'll have more time to take me to the mall," Mom said. "When the day comes, I plan to bury him near Nordstrom so I have a reason to visit him each week."

Wim and I chuckled, but my heart dropped. I was fully conscious of my emotional and financial dependence on my parents; I couldn't fathom living without them.

"It's going to be harder for your generation to live as comfortably as we have. When we were your age, once a week your mom and I would go out for a five-dollar steak dinner at Monte's Restaurant, the only splurge we allowed ourselves because we were saving money for this." He indicated the house with a sweep of his hand.

He retold the same story I had heard many times before—about how the year I was born, in preparation for my arrival, my parents began the process of building their custom home in

Downey. Unable to afford to buy their dream house, and unwilling to settle for a starter home, they purchased for $12,500 a two-thirds-acre lot with towering eucalyptus trees a few minutes' drive from my grandparents' house. It sat in a neighborhood of emerging California ranch-style homes, also on large lots. My parents used to picnic on the property with my older brother and sister, then two and five years old.

Two or three years later, they had saved enough money for a down payment on a loan and were able to build the house. It cost $65,000 and, next to their kids, remained their greatest source of pride: a large, four-bedroom, three-and-a-half bath, single-story home sitting high on a hill, its tall front doors flanked by contemporary white stone. The shallow-pitched, simple A-frame roofline created a distinctive vaulted family room ceiling—a feature that, in 1966, was ahead of its time. A simple marble-tiled fireplace surround and hearth were designed in harmony with the marble entryway.

Living in a big house, I had always vacillated between pride and self-consciousness. Our house awed my childhood friends, most of whom lived on the other side of town in small tract homes. They called our small but glamorous powder room "the fancy bathroom." I too was enamored of its gold gilded faucet with crystal knobs, flocked white wallpaper, and embellished gold soap dish and decorative rose-shaped hand soaps. At a time when a bar of green soap on a piece of rope was something special, using our powder room in all its regal splendor was akin to peeing at the Palace of Versailles.

Now here I sat, nearly twenty years later, around the same glass-top table where my family used to convene for dinner each night and recapture the day's events. As I watched my parents, both of them sitting at their designated places at the table—Mom closest to the counter so she could easily serve and clear, Dad directly across from her, and me in between—I felt a pang in my chest, hoping that saving money to build a house would be an experience Wim and I could share with our own children someday.

My dad's voice broke into my reverie. "Arlene and I always lived within our means. I would caution you and Janie to do the same." He looked at Wim. I nodded in confirmation. Of course we would. *We are a sensible couple*, I thought proudly.

The rest of the conversation revolved around whether the leather sofa from his office would fit through our apartment door.

CHAPTER 13: WANTED: KICK-ASS KITCHEN

Raymond Ave, Rye – July 2007

E thel Vanguard had the reputation of being difficult, but word around town was she designed beautiful kitchens. I tracked her down in an industrial park near the local airport— an unlikely location, I thought, for a kitchen-design service. My daughter Paige and I entered the nondescript office building, and a receptionist buzzed us in through the large glass doors. A few minutes later I was shaking hands with a Phyllis Diller look-alike: a wild-haired bleach blonde, her makeup layered as heavily as a Sunday-night lasagna. She was dressed like a diva in a designer suit and high heels and was bedazzled in impressive jewels—big diamond studs and a massive diamond solitaire engagement ring. Rows of kitchen plans hung down behind her on metal racks like sides of beef at the butcher.

Ethel's assistant whisked Paige off to a room with a video player and a bag of cookies. I followed Ethel and her trail of cologne into the main showroom, where she plied me with coffee, donuts, and her best sales pitch. She started with a seminar in cab-inetmaking, during which she explained the difference between inset and overlay cabinets—the only perceptible variation to me being the $10,000 difference in price.

"Do you want glazed cabinets, hon?"

"Uh, that sounds nice," I said.

"There is an upcharge for that." She moved on to other seemingly endless options: Corian, granite, or marble counters? Wood or tile floor? Porcelain, metal, or glass backsplash? She romanced me with glossy photos of award-winning kitchens she had designed.

It may have been her musky perfume, but I soon found myself falling under her spell. She led me over to another section of the showroom, where, like a game show assistant displaying Doors Number 1, 2, and 3, she spread out her arm toward three different kitchens, each one more stunning than the last. She asked what I wanted: The old-country charm of the Tuscan kitchen? The simple, sleek lines of the modern kitchen?

"I'm leaning toward the traditional kitchen, but..." This was all happening so fast.

"Well if you like this traditional kitchen, we'll just replicate our display. We can do it just like that!" she said, snapping her fingers.

Instantly, I understood. Her shop was a factory of kitchen modules, where the same three models were cranked out over and over. But I didn't want a "presto" kitchen. A kitchen, to me, was a work of art. I didn't want a lithograph; I wanted an original. And like every other aspect of my house, I wanted to help create it—to experience the joy of agonizing over every last detail. I collected my daughter, along with another donut, and hit the road.

●——————●

My next interview was with a designer named Tom.

Tom wore a blue button-down shirt and navy tie; his gray hair was shorn close to his head like he was a spring lamb. He explained in great detail his products and services and handed me a steady stream of brochures.

"So, is there anything special you're looking for?" he asked finally, looking at me as if he were seeing me for the first time.

I quickly discovered I wasn't comfortable discussing my culinary desires with a male kitchen designer. I'd grown up in a time when the kitchen was a woman's arena, where dads wandered in only to replenish their Heinekens. I told Tom about my storage needs and expressed my desire for a Tupperware drawer, a special place to keep all those plastic storage containers and their elusive lids. But Tom didn't want to talk about kitchen storage. He seemed only concerned with cabinets, counters, and floors. When I tried to steer the conversation back to Tupperware, he nodded politely, glanced at his watch, and told me he had another appointment.

•————•

Then I met Joan, who had designed some of the most beautiful kitchens and bathrooms in town. Joan was a middle-aged blonde who wore a single strand of pearls over her cashmere sweater. She had a sophisticated wholesomeness about her; she was the type of woman you could imagine spending afternoons baking soufflés and enjoying evenings at the opera.

At our initial meeting in her small studio in Scarsdale, New York, she asked casually, "Do you know what kind of kitchen you want?"

Sitting at her hand-carved wood pedestal table, I plunked down a red vinyl binder crammed with magazine pages capturing every aspect of kitchen design from flooring to countertops. This binder was the cousin to my black book, which by now had become so crowded with inspiration that tiny cracks had erupted along its once-pristine spine.

Since meeting with Ethel Vanguard, I'd attended every kitchen-tour fundraiser within a sixty-mile radius and scoured every kitchen-design magazine on the racks until I'd discovered precisely the look I was after: a blend of traditional and contemporary styles through simple lines, neutral colors, and varied textures. The term for it was "transitional," and it was to become the design scheme for our entire house.

"It looks like you've brought some pictures to show me." Joan smiled at me and nodded toward the binder, apparently undaunted by the thought of perusing a catalog so enormous I was sure the table would give way any second under its weight.

Joan seemed so relaxed, I probably could have said I wanted a disco ball hanging from my kitchen ceiling and she wouldn't have batted an eye.

When I mentioned my Tupperware-drawer idea, she said, "I think that's smart. Tupperware is one of those things we use regularly but never seem to have a good place for."

"Exactly!" I said.

"Your kitchen should be designed to fulfill your unique needs. I have a client who loves to bake, so I designed a special cabinet for her to store her baking supplies, things like flour, sugar, and baking soda," she said brightly.

"Yes. That totally makes sense." Unlike the other designers I'd met, she seemed open to the idea of customizing our kitchen to our specifications.

"This won't be your mother's cookie-cutter kitchen," she said.

"Good." I laughed. "Because my mother wouldn't settle for a cookie-cutter kitchen." I thought of the hidden pull-out cutting board beneath my parents' kitchen countertop, custom designed for them, and finally felt understood.

Every one of Joan's kitchens were custom built, every cabinet handmade. Of course, this made her designs some of the most expensive in the area. But as I ran my fingers along the smooth edge of the two-tone walnut pedestal table, I was suddenly reminded of my mother's favorite pair of Ferragamo black-and-white wing-tip spectator pumps in Italian leather. I still remembered when she purchased them, could picture her admiring her feet in the mirror while I sat beside her, swinging my ten-year-old legs to the live music of a tuxedo-clad pianist playing soft jazz on a Steinway grand just a few yards away.

"Aren't they beautiful?" she said. "A little more than I wanted to spend."

I watched her gently slip off the designer shoes, insert them back into their protective drawstring pouches, and place them in the box.

"But it's better to pay more for something that will last."

She pulled out her credit card as I followed her to the register.

"I think you'll really like Joan's kitchen designs," I told Wim later, and my prophecy came true. He was floored by her design. But he was more floored by her price.

"You could have a new Mercedes-Benz for that," he said.

"I'd rather have a kick-ass kitchen," I said.

CHAPTER 14: UP IN FLAMES

Downey, CA – December 1990

I can still picture Wim's shoes lined up with geometric perfection at the foot of his neatly made bed. I remember the special five-course meal he prepared for my visit to Switzerland—the one I hoped would allow us to establish where we stood in our relationship and determine whether we had a real future together.

I remember the two of us sitting in his barely eat-in kitchen, playfully examining the Caesar salad, the hairy-looking dark anchovies making it seem as if someone had lost an eyebrow in the mixed greens. The smell of chicken roasting in the oven—how we scurried down to the cellar for a bottle of wine, got swept away in an intimate moment, and returned to find the kitchen smoking, the bird engulfed in flames. Our side trip to Paris, where I took a nap in our hotel room and awakened to find Wim standing over me, wet with rain and holding a bouquet of white roses. The dinner party at the home of his friend Patsy, our embarrassment when she greeted us with surprise—she wasn't expecting us (we'd forgotten to RSVP)—our humiliation when she insisted we stay even though she didn't have enough chairs to seat us, and how we spent the entire meal perched on a suitcase. And how, young and in love, standing on Patsy's balcony later that evening, watching New Year's fireworks, wrapped in Wim's arms as brilliant bursts fell over the city, I felt like we were a pair of stars, perfectly aligned in the night sky.

For more than two years since the summer we'd said goodbye in Portugal, I'd been tormented by loneliness. I tried to bury myself in my studies in an effort to fill what was missing, only to find myself distracted by the very things I missed: our long walks in the woods, our candlelight dinners in his apartment, our lazy afternoons together in bed. I longed to be near him, to hold him, to touch him. I longed to breathe in the musk scent of his Ralph Lauren cologne: woody, herbal, and spicy. I longed for him to undress me and lay me across his duvet, my body naked, cushioned by the downy layer. I longed for him to map the constellations on the curve of my back, to feel his fingers trailing the small dark dots of Ursa Major over my northern sky.

Here we were, two people deeply in love and happy, but we were apart, which made me feel depressed and alone. The only thing that brought comfort was when he'd remind me that we were both looking at the same moon, just as we had our last night together in Lagos.

Like any couple, we argued—only unlike other couples, our arguments strained our relationship *and* our wallets. In one night we racked up an $800 phone bill, most of the conversation spent feuding. Each minute that passed reminded me of a dollar sign popping up on a vintage cash register, time burning a hole in my pocket, burning up money I was trying to save for our future together.

Over time, our visits doubled, our phone bills tripled, and my heartache quadrupled. I was consumed by thoughts and dreams of him. I saw his face on students I passed in the hallway, on billboards and TV commercials. I read and reread his letters.

Wim had dreams, and not all of them included me. He wanted to travel, a prospect that, in my mind, threatened our relationship. His ambivalence was forcing me to step back and look at where I was in my life and what I wanted: A husband. A child. A house.

Then, finally, Wim announced that he would be leaving Switzerland in the coming summer. He would make plans to come to LA. In my mind, I started to make my own plan—to make a home with him.

• ———— •

It was the beginning of summer, and dusk was hovering in Los Angeles; in Zurich, the sun hadn't yet risen.

I picked up the phone, surprised to hear Wim's voice on the other end. "What are you doing up?" I said. "It's only five o'clock in the morning for you." I leaned against the headboard in my childhood bedroom.

"There's something I need to tell you," Wim said.

"What's wrong?"

Outside the window, two great horned owls called to each other with deep, soft hoots, *hoo-hoo, hoo-hoo*.

"I'm not ready to move back to the US. I booked a round-the-world trip for a year."

His words hung like a dense fog, heavy and tangible—the kind we'd once driven through at eighty miles per hour on the Autobahn to Austria. The kind where visibility is cut down within seconds, resulting in disastrous pileups.

"I'm leaving for Asia next month," he said.

I stared, speechless, into a patch of white-and-pink-checkered wallpaper until it blended into a fuzzy haze. If the owls hooted, I didn't notice.

He said he had purchased a one-way, nonrefundable ticket: Switzerland to Morocco, Morocco to India, India to China, and on and on. The trip would take a year, or longer. He planned to end his trip in New York.

This didn't make sense. Hadn't he already made a commitment—to me?

I pictured him lying on his bed, the receiver on his ear tethered to the cradle on his nightstand, his head resting against his wood headboard.

"We're in different places in our lives," he continued. "You've finished graduate school and gotten a job; you've moved in with your parents to save money."

"And you want to travel the world," I said sharply.

"Janie, you know I love you, but this is something I've been dreaming of for a long time. If I don't do it now, I never will."

• —— •

I wrote Wim letters. I called, desperate to change his mind, but also desperate to not sound desperate. If there was ever a tightrope between preservation and breakup, I was walking it.

I talked to Shayna and lamented to my parents.

"It's not fair," I complained to my father as we walked the hills around my parents' neighborhood, our daily routine—the only thing I felt I could depend on anymore.

"Life's not fair," my dad said, offering his standard-issue response, though his voice was not without sympathy.

He pointed to a tree with dark oval leaves and small white flowers. "Do you remember what kind of tree that is?"

I scanned the reserve in my brain and started ticking off flowering trees he'd pointed out over the years on walks, drives, trips together—magnolia, crepe myrtle, plum—and before I knew it I was thinking of Wim and me on a hill in an apple orchard near his Swiss apartment, stretched out on a blanket, looking up at clusters of pink blossoms against a buttermilk sky. "I wish you could stay here," he murmured. I could feel the warmth of his touch under my blouse, his fingers gliding upward.

"The blossoms can be white or pink," my father hinted, his words reeling me back to the present, back to the game we'd been playing since I was a child, testing my knowledge of the world: nature, politics, culture, and religion. He loved to fill in the gaps with his own encyclopedic explanations. Then, it came to me.

"Dogwood," I said eagerly. I still wanted to impress him with the right answer, even at twenty-three years old.

•———•

A week later, Wim called again. I sat at my desk, a stack of his letters beside me, and fingered an envelope as I listened. I'd just finished reading a letter dated August 1988, the first he'd ever written me.

> *Janie,*
> *Let me ask you a question. Who ever said, "Parting is such sweet sorrow?" I'm only asking because nothing about saying goodbye to you was sweet. Well that's not all true. Your lips were. What I mean is we talked about being sad but watching you leave was truly saddening. It was only one week ago that Shayna, Max, you and I were in Lagos. I've been thinking about you this last week. Wishing you were still here. I thought about how*

you wanted to go to Granada and while I was at the Alhambra I could only imagine what it would have been like to share that afternoon with you.

Enough about could have beens. Let's talk fact. Lagos was beautiful—not just the place but everything. You really made that weekend an unforgettable one. It was a paradise and I'm glad we got to share it together. How long was it that we actually knew each other?

I turned the envelope over and over in my hands, thinking about how people could enter our lives so suddenly, and exit just as quickly. Could two years of love and commitment vanish in a single conversation? Wim would tell me how he valued his independence, reminding me how in high school he'd waited tables at the Grist Mill to save money for a car—a 1974 used Volkswagen Scirocco, old and battered, but it got him where he needed to go. How he worked his way through college at Huntington Plaza selling cigars, fine clothing, and accessories at a men's haberdashery, a word I had never heard of until I met him; how he liked his freedom and didn't want to be stifled. How he loved me but couldn't let go of his dream to see the world. I waited for the words, "It's over."

Instead, I heard him say, "I'll move back, but on one condition."

I held my breath.

"If I'm going to give up my life here, I want a commitment from you. I want to live together."

I jumped up from my chair and paced the carpet as far as the phone cord would allow. To the ceiling, I mouthed, "Thank you!"

CHAPTER 15: CONSPICUOUS CONSTRUCTION

Raymond Ave, Rye – August 2006

When Wim and I first moved to Rye, we had to choose whether to live in Rye Borough or Rye Township. Even though they shared a public library, a post office, and even a common zip code, the two sections of Rye were divided into two governments. They were also divided in spirit and had been fierce rivals for generations, each municipality fighting (in the hockey rink, sometimes literally) for respect. I'd heard you could have had a Borough–Township game of tiddlywinks and it would be sold out.

The Township was historically a place where farmers lived on large properties and tended dairy farms and cattle, but those farms had since been replaced by luxurious new homes on large lots. Borough residents, considered sophisticated city folk, were willing to tolerate tighter living space for the perks of convenient access to town, including a train-station parking pass that town hall reserved for Borough residents only.

The competition had mellowed in recent years, but an underlying mutual feeling of contempt remained—despite the fact that both sections were equally filled with hedge fund managers, parents paying for private tutors for their children, and people vacationing in Africa and Alaska. A Township friend said to me once, "I had to get out of the Borough. The houses are packed so tight I couldn't retrieve my morning newspaper without listening to my neighbor rattle on every morning about her dog's thyroid problem." A Borough friend, meanwhile, scoffed, "I hear Townie women don't wear sweatpants—they wear 'yoga apparel.'"

When we were house hunting for the second time, we had to make the choice again. Staying in the Borough would allow us to continue to enjoy the community feeling that a tighter-knit environment lends; moving to the Township, with its sprawling acreage, would give us the space we craved. We wanted a larger house, but we valued being close enough to neighbors that we could chat from porch to porch and watch the kids play in their front yards, things that make you feel like you're connected.

Ultimately, we decided to stay in the Borough, holding out for a rare large property, thinking we could have it all. On Lexington Avenue, we'd literally be living on the border, between Borough conservatism and Township flash. While many of my peers had upgraded to larger homes, some of my closest friends lived in homes that were quite modest, and the potential scale of our new house made me self-conscious.

I feared being judged for having a basement that was as big as some of my friends' homes. "She used to be so down-to-earth," I imagined them saying. They'd make assumptions, wrongly believing that I'd adopted a new image to match my conspicuous construction, that I'd trade in our neighborhood walks together for private personal trainers and substitute volunteer time for a time-share in Bermuda. When we first started talking about renovating, I worried that I'd lose my friends.

I don't know why. I had a tight-knit group of friends I'd grown close with over the years; hanging out on the school playground together, pushing our babies on the swing set, and watching our kids climb on the jungle gym had bonded us together. We'd exchanged books, traded recipes, and shared carpools.

I loved that my friends didn't care how big or small their—or anyone else's—houses were. However, I thought some of them were shocked by what we spent on our Lexington Avenue home. So the self-doubt began to creep in.

We would appear wealthier as we built our big house, but in reality we were stretched thinner than ever. I wasn't trying to reinvent myself—just my home. I'd always told my kids that "what matters isn't what you have but how you act toward others." But if I was being honest with myself, I believed it was really both.

Would I start putting on airs once I moved to an area where the culture was trumping the neighbor's latest acquisition? For the zillionth time, I asked myself if we should have stayed put. But then, in my mind, I saw our Raymond Avenue house with its small kitchen and no garage, my parents having to stay at a Courtyard by Marriott twenty minutes away. I heard my mother: *Maybe in your next house you'll have a mudroom.* I heard my son's school friend: *Where's the rest of your house?*

I told myself we made the right decision.

CHAPTER 16: A ROUGH START

Rosemead, CA – September 1992

I t was a warm, sunny morning. Cotton clouds drifted over our heads; a black crow cawed from a nearby power line. I stood crouching over a tomato plant, grimacing at a four-inch, phallus-shaped creature that looked like it had been designed for a science fiction movie.

"Last one," Wim said with satisfaction as he took a gloved hand and plucked off a fat, ugly hornworm enjoying a destructive meal at our garden "salad bar." I stood ready with a disposable jar in hand and watched him drop the wriggling insect inside to join its companions. For hours we'd lost ourselves in an obsessive game of hunt and pluck.

"How many is that?" He removed his gloves and set them down on a yellow wire garden seat.

"Six," I said, relieved that the worms were inside the jar and order was restored to our little patio garden. I observed them tumbling and clinging together, desperate to escape.

I picked up a mallet and struck a new stake into the tomato pot, trying not to hit any roots.

"I can't believe we started this thing from seed." Wim gestured to the vine that had grown past his own shoulders, beyond the five-foot stake. The bent plant, weighted down with shiny clusters of red-ripe heirloom tomatoes, leaned over, yearning for reinforcement. "When I was a kid, we used to give our tomatoes a head start by growing them in small containers under artificial light in our basement until it warmed up outside." His words were tinged with nostalgia.

"It's strange to think that you grew up with basements."

"It's strange to think you didn't."

"Where do these worms even come from?" I peered into the jar to get a good look at one—the V-shaped marks on each side, the tiny black horn on its hind end—then handed Wim the jar.

His lips curved down and he stroked his chin, pondering the mysteries of the tomato hornworm. "No idea," he answered.

We had yet to figure out that the stunning, hummingbird-like moths we often admired in the late afternoon, unrolling their proboscises like party noisemakers to sip nectar from our deep-lobed petunias, had evolved from these very larvae.

I silently mused over how something could appear out of nowhere—an ocean wave, a shooting star, a flashback, a romance. A thought emerged out of the blue, prompting me to remind Wim about our dinner plans. "Don't forget, we're having dinner with the Greenbergs and the Kahns in Santa Monica tonight."

Wim's head fell back, his eyes closing with annoyance. "Can't they come here?"

"To Rosemead? And eat where, In-N-Out Burger?"

He frowned. "I'd rather do that than traipse across LA County just to hang out with friends."

"They're your friends," I reminded him.

"Then they'll understand."

I knew his irritation stemmed not just from the inconvenience of long-distance friendships but also from his growing disenchantment with Los Angeles. Wim had left Zurich to build a life with me in California with no car and no cash, only a suitcase in hand. He had left his conservative East Coast roots and arrived in an unfamiliar place where snow was only on TV, earthquakes were a real threat, and Barbie actually lived in Malibu. He couldn't fathom kids surfing, grown men skateboarding, grandparents sporting tattoos, or, most important, raising a family in Los Angeles.

Hoping to temper his displeasure, I told him I'd made reservations at the Greek restaurant he liked, the one with the marinated lamb kabobs. His look told me the restaurant didn't matter.

"It'll take us an hour to drive there, and that's assuming we don't get caught in any crossfire on the way."

He was being facetious, but there had recently been a rash of drive-by shootings in Los Angeles, and crime seemed to be creeping closer and closer to home. Driving to my parents' house recently, we'd witnessed two policemen holding down a man at gunpoint in his driveway, his hands cuffed behind his back. I'd been so shaken by the sight that I had begun to carry mace on my keychain.

"I hate the traffic as much as you do," I said, "but Saturday's better than weekday traffic."

Wim looked frustrated. "It's more than that."

A feeling of apprehension stirred inside of me. I knew what was coming. We'd performed this kabuki dance since he'd moved to LA, and we always ended up back in the same place. Marriage, it was turning out, wasn't the Cinderella fairy tale I'd grown up believing it to be.

I often wondered why young people weren't better prepared for marriage—why Home Economics required us to learn how to make snickerdoodles (cookies a three-year-old could bake unsupervised) and seventh-grade woodshop required us to build birdhouses. Why couldn't high school have offered Marriage 101, where I'd have learned how to be a more active listener, to say "You seem a little frustrated" rather than "You're being ridiculous."

"I've lived here for two years and—"

"You don't like it, I know," I interrupted. "But this is home."

"This is where we live," he corrected.

This is where I've built my life, I thought but didn't say. How could I? He had built his life too—in Switzerland.

"You don't know what it's like to leave everything behind. In Zurich I had my life together. I had a good job, I had connections, I traveled, I had my own apartment—"

My mind flashed to the year Wim moved in with me—and my parents. Wim slept on one side of the house and I slept on the other, an arrangement that often included one of us creeping past my mother, asleep on the couch late at night, and lasted for an entire year, until we got our own digs in Rosemead.

"You've got your life together now. You're in graduate school. Soon you'll be working," I said hopefully, all too aware of the burden of expectation he felt to "make something of himself." It was an expectation set by all of us—me, my parents, and Wim— that had spilled over into pressure. Wim's goal had been to travel around the world. Instead, he'd moved to a place he hated and had spent the past two years struggling to find the right career path, all of which had been causing us to have the same arguments over and over again.

"I'm just saying it's been hard. I'm not happy, okay?" Wim frowned. "This isn't what I expected my life to be." He flicked the glass jar with his finger and knocked the caterpillars down. Each time they gained an inch, he knocked them down again.

"Wow," I said, taken aback by his blunt statement. "Not happy? I know you had a rough start, but—"

LISA TOGNOLA ❧ 115

"A rough start?" His jaw tightened. "It was the middle of a recession when I first moved here." His voice was rising. "I remember feeling like everyone around me—all of our friends—had their act together, going to work in suits, practicing law. And what was I doing? Data entry. It was humiliating—one of the worst periods of my life," he yelled, his angry hazel eyes fixed on mine. His fingers were clamped so tightly on the jar, I feared it would shatter in his hand.

"Wim, keep your voice down." I cast a quick glance over the patio railing. I heard our next-door neighbor, Judy, turn down her TV.

"I don't give a crap if Judy hears me. I've listened to worse things come out of her." Tilting the uncapped glass jar back as if it were a grenade catapult, he turned his body and pitched the tomato worms toward her patio.

"Wim!"

A spray of live projectiles went flying over the railing like siege weapons. One landed on the frayed edge of Judy's faded red umbrella above a cigarette-littered table, where it dangled precariously over a plastic lounge chair.

Wim stood there clutching the jar, now empty of its contents. His expression was a cross between anger and bemusement. Before I could even open my mouth he answered, "Because I felt like it."

"What the hell, Wim?" I said. Hostility was an emotion I'd observed more and more from him lately. His mood had always been erratic; in the past, that was linked to his appeal. I found his moodiness mysterious, intriguing, even sexy. But he was starting to scare me.

"I have every right to be angry," he snapped. "I've bent over backward for you. You haven't had to sacrifice anything in this relationship." I could see the exasperation in his face, hear the pain and resentment in his voice.

"So it's my fault that you're unhappy?"

"That's not what I said." He paused for a moment. "Look…" His voice dropped down a couple of decibels. "I've tried to make this work. It's just not getting any better." He stared vacantly at the empty jar.

Living in LA or our marriage? I wondered. I suddenly felt panicky. "What are you saying?" I asked, so frightened that I could hardly stand to meet his eyes.

His face was tense as he stared at me. "I don't know what I'm saying." He turned away.

My fight-or-flight instinct activated instantly; I reacted like a grazing zebra that sees a lion closing in for the kill. I fled inside our apartment, barreled into our bedroom, and flung myself down on the bed, squeezing my eyes shut. A lump formed in my throat that burned when I swallowed, and sadness settled into my heart. Blinking back the tears, I sat up and picked up the phone.

I dialed the Northern California number I had memorized since Shayna and I met at a Jewish summer retreat for young adults six years earlier. Though we only spoke a few times a month, she and I shared a tightly woven bond, like sisters. She'd been with me when I'd broken my arm. She'd been with me when I'd first fallen in love with Wim. She'd been a bridesmaid at our wedding.

"Shayna…" My voice cracked.

"Janie? What's wrong?"

"Wim and I…" I gasped through my tears. I tried to continue, but a cry shook through me.

"Wim and you what?" she pressed.

I could picture Shayna's face, her dark features and bronzed complexion. I imagined her thick-lashed walnut brown eyes encouraging me to continue.

"We got into an argument and he said he doesn't like living

here but I never really took him seriously, and now what if he leaves—"

"Janie, he's not going to leave you. Just slow down and take a deep breath."

I inhaled deeply and slowly let out my breath. "When I think about it, our lives have been built around my school, my friends, and my family, and . . . I don't think I've realized how hard it's been for him."

"I can understand it being hard for him. He moved to California not knowing a soul besides you. He didn't know what he wanted to do with his life—just that he wanted to spend it with you. He knew that when he first met you. I mean, when he first met *us*." She laughed.

I was staring off into the distance, watching a palm tree sway in the breeze outside my window, remembering, when Shayna's voice startled me back into the present.

"Everything's going to be okay, Janie. Do you remember the note you gave Wim when you said goodbye to him at the train station?"

"He still carries it in his wallet." I smiled. "My lipstick kiss has faded, but you can still read the words: 'Until we meet again . . .'"

"You're destined to be together," she told me. "You just have to figure out *where* you're supposed to be together."

After we hung up, my eyes fell upon a framed wedding photo on the dresser—Wim and me, newly married, walking hand in hand down the aisle, our wide grins conveying hope and trust.

I heard a quiet knock.

Wim entered our bedroom. I wondered whether he had come to give me an apology, or to collect one.

CHAPTER 17: GRANDMA'S DILL PICKLES

Lexington Ave, Rye – May 2007

It was late Saturday afternoon—weeks before the teardown. Wim and I stood in the driveway watching four volunteers from Habitat for Humanity haul off plumbing supplies, light fixtures, and operable appliances until they had completely stripped the house of every last valuable.

One of the men carried out a stainless steel sink he'd wrestled free from our kitchen counter. The sight conjured up a vision of my Grandma Rose, standing at her yellow Formica kitchen counter making dill pickles. I could see the mason jars lined up in neat rows, and my grandma covering the glass jars with pieces of waxed paper that she'd washed and reused, then screwing the lids on tight. She came from a generation that used things until they were worn out. She shamelessly darned socks, tore unsalvageable clothes into reusable rags, and always squeezed the toothpaste from the bottom to wring out every last bit. When she bought a chicken, nothing was wasted. Even the carcass was boiled for chicken stock. She couldn't have fathomed destroying a functional house.

So how could I? It felt less like a choice and more like an inevitability that I'd finally caught up to. Having the perfect house had been my dream for so long that the idea itself had become an unstoppable force, powerful enough to lure me into its grip, even if it meant compromising my values.

"A few more weeks and this won't be here." Wim gestured to the house with a sweep of his hand.

My stomach churned with guilt and regret. I pulled my thumbnail out from between my teeth and gave him an unconvincing thumbs-up.

"What is it?" he asked.

"I just hope we made the right decision." We'd both been raised in homes our parents had built. But neither of our parents had purchased and knocked down an existing home to do so. It all just felt wrong.

Since we'd moved to Rye it had become more common for builders to bulldoze older houses and replace them with luxurious spec homes. But it was rare for individual homeowners to tear down a house and build a custom home from scratch. Most people didn't want the headache, but mostly they didn't want the expense.

Yet here we were, ripping down a home to get what we wanted, where we wanted it, and it made me feel both ashamed and misunderstood. It wasn't just a matter of conspicuous consumption. To people who were passionate about preserving our neighborhood's original character, our teardown was sacrilege, and I worried they'd look on in contempt. We'd already managed to tick off the Zambonis with the fence thing.

It was a problem I'd long suffered, looking at myself from the eyes of others, measuring my self-worth based on others' perceptions. I wanted to assure them all that we were going to build a home that would fit with the integrity of the neighborhood and wouldn't be too large for the lot or eliminate all of the trees. But what was I going to do, drive around shouting it through a bullhorn? It was a worry that kept me up at night, nagging at me like a garment tag scratching my neck.

Yet the more Wim and I had talked about it, the more convinced I'd become that it was the best decision. "We live in a desirable area with older houses and no open land," Wim had said. "If we want to be in this neighborhood and the house doesn't meet our needs, then it's the most logical solution."

But now, as I watched two volunteers cart off a gently used refrigerator that we'd rejected because we wanted new appliances, I imagined my grandma grimacing, hands to cheeks, rocking her head side to side in disapproval.

"You hope we made the right decision?" Wim responded, his demeanor changed. There was an edge to his voice when he said, "Janie, please let's not do this now."

I knew it wasn't the right time to have this conversation. But I wanted reassurance. I willed him to affirm for me that we were doing the right thing. I gave him a pleading look.

He softened. "Look, we ran the numbers and it makes sense. Renovating wouldn't get us everything we want. We wouldn't be able to add to the mudroom or build out the basement. It makes more sense to spend a little more and get what we want. Can we just accept that and enjoy this day?"

"You're right, you're right," I said, using repetition to convince myself.

CHAPTER 18: BULLETS AND DUMMIES

Lexington Ave, Rye – May 2007

The sound of bullets firing shattered an otherwise peaceful afternoon. My kids and I huddled quietly in the side yard under the narrow shade of a small pine tree, watching the chaotic scene unfold. I spied dark-suited men descending upon our house, surrounding the place, crouching behind fences, and hiding along the sidewalk and bushes. They wore heavy body armor—ballistic vests, helmets with face shields, and gloves—their backs, sleeves, and helmets marked "POLICE" in white lettering. The six armed officers, members of the Rye SWAT team and Rye Police Department, stepped out with an arsenal of shotguns, sub-machine guns, and long-range rifles slung over their shoulders. Each wore a hand-gun on his leg.

From their command post in the front corner of our yard, two officers moved forward quickly, weapons drawn. I heard only fragments: "*Police . . . search warrant!*"

"Look at the smoke, look at the smoke." Our son Hunter seemed more awestruck than nervous as he pointed to the pollen-like haze of yellow smoke billowing out from an upstairs bedroom. In an eight-year-old's eyes, these cops were exciting cartoon ninjas come to life.

"It smells like fireworks!" Paige shouted.

"Shh!" I placed a finger to my lips to quiet my daughter, but her eyes were focused on the officers who had suddenly left their post by the old, weathered split-rail fence and moved toward the house.

We heard more gunfire—three loud shots, followed by two more—warning shots fired to flush the suspect from his hiding place. A dog barked mercilessly in the background.

Hunter jabbed at the yellow-streaked air with his finger and pointed out more men across the street. Cars slowed as curious onlookers passed our house. I took a few steps forward to get a better view of the men, but the hot sun forced me back into the shade.

Paige gasped. "They're breaking the windows!"

I swiveled back around, the sound of shattering glass reminding me we were no longer in control of our own house.

More shouting came from inside: "Show me your hands!" Two shots rang out. "Police! Show me your hands! Down on the floor!" Gunshots again.

A man exited the house, his hands raised over his head. "Stop shooting," he said.

Two men made a diagonal move to a large oak in the front yard while a point man carrying a tactical shield led the others to the back of the house. The officers moved snake-like in a single-file line, weapons ready. They halted at the back door.

With several thrusts of a battering ram, the point man broke the door open. The loud boom caused my heart to leap out of my chest. He rushed in; the others followed. I felt my color drain as

I imagined a hostage lying dead, facedown, wearing khakis and a bloody T-shirt, his body sprawled across the kitchen floor.

Seconds later, they opened fire, firing five rounds. "Search warrant! Police! Show me your hands! Police, show me your hands!" We heard the sound of glass shattering and banging on doors. More shots echoed from inside the house.

After a few minutes, the police retreated. The air fell silent. I closed my eyes and reveled in the absence of noise. Birds began to chirp. Things slowly returned to normal.

Just a short time ago, we hadn't even known that Rye had a SWAT team. Now, staring at our battered house, I remembered the conversation we'd had with the police department after we learned from the demolition company that they were looking for vacant buildings to conduct hands-on training in. Sergeant Gladstone had said the trainings covered such potential situations as hostage rescues, barricaded gunmen, and practice using distraction devices he referred to as "flash-bangs." The police training would involve "room-to-room searches and maybe knocking down some of the interior doors," he said, but no live ammunition.

His description had not prepared me for this. The past twenty minutes had been like watching an episode of *Homeland*.

Sergeant Gladstone approached. "Mrs. Margolis," he said with a nod.

"How did it go?" I asked.

His dark eyebrows gave his face, red with heat, a menacing look; lines of sweat trickled down his cheeks. He began to remove his helmet clamps. "They were a little rough on the place."

He'd told me there weren't a lot of private homeowners tearing down houses in Rye. "And the ones that do don't usually know they can serve their community by letting us train there," he'd said.

"Nothing says community like a hostage rescue," I'd said.

• —— •

After the armored SWAT vehicles drove off, my kids scampered into the house. The walls were riddled with bullet holes—the result of an afternoon session of gangster-style indoor target practice. They scrambled from room to room, picking up the rubber bullets that had ricocheted through our house and scooping into their hands as many as they could carry.

"Can we keep these?" Hunter asked, nodding to the bullet-torn silhouettes that populated the walls.

"Sure," I said. They would be the only remnant of the house as it now was after we destroyed it.

• —— •

The police training was so successful that we agreed to let the fire department use the house as well. I couldn't help but hope that if the neighbors saw us putting the house to good use, it might mitigate any disapproval about us destroying it.

But things grew complicated.

The town required that we sign a contract that said that if anyone were injured on the property, Rye would not be liable, *we* would.

"There's no way I'm going to assume liability," Wim said. "I'm going to talk to Fire Chief Nate."

We'd known Nate since his days as a volunteer fire fighter. He was a friendly guy with curly bright copper hair that licked the edges of his helmet like flames, as if his hair were on fire. Over the years he'd responded to countless emergency calls at our house involving natural gas odors, medical incidents, misdialed numbers, and, on one embarrassing occasion, a flaming salmon.

Finally, after a week of negotiation, Rye borough's attorney agreed to change the language. For days, the local fire battalion used our house as a temporary training site. Despite the advance warning, the drills moved the neighborhood into a state of panic every time simulated smoke billowed out our windows. Training culminated in a multi-town emergency bonanza that included a dozen fire trucks, half a dozen police cars, and two ambulances, the flashing lights of the vehicles bouncing off the home's white siding with cinematic flare. Power saws hummed, glass shattered, and men shouted as fire fighters cut holes in the roof, breached walls, and knocked out windows. A red fire truck was parked on our front lawn, an extension ladder thrown to a second-floor window pluming with heavy smoke, and water shot from a hose line stretched across the green grass.

From my perch near the curb I heard someone yell, "Help!" from the second-floor window. Seconds later, a tall, burly fire-fighter was climbing up the ladder. I watched him hoist a man in his arms, cradle him like a baby, and slowly make his way down the ladder. My hands were damp and sweaty.

Wim emerged from his car and mouthed the words, "Oh, shit." He ran across the yard to where the EMTs had rushed to the victim's aid and were administering artificial respiration through a plastic mask. "I knew someone was going to get hurt!" he said, drawing closer. He was on his tiptoes, trying to catch a glimpse of the man sprawled out on the grass, his eyes despairing. "What the hell happened to his legs?"

I craned my neck to get a better view, but I couldn't see through the wall of EMTs working collectively to resuscitate the victim.

Wim's eyes cut over to Nate and back to the legless man. "Nate, what happened to that guy?" he cried.

Nate chuckled. "That guy is Dummy Dan, our search and rescue dummy."

"Dummy?" Wim echoed. He closed his eyes and took a breath. "I didn't know search and rescue was part of today's drill."

"Well, now you know." Nate grinned.

CHAPTER 19: HURT AND STUPID

Raymond Ave, Rye – June 2007

Tension had been rising at Wim's work. The previous week, when he'd returned from a trip to London, he'd told me that two of his company's hedge funds had collapsed, something about an emergence of subprime loan losses on banks.

It was embarrassing, even shameful, that I had only a vague understanding of his job, other than that he securitized loans for a living. Sometimes over dinner or a drink I'd ask him how one of his deals was going. But before long, without realizing it, he'd be talking about business concepts I didn't understand until I felt like I was back in Algebra I, where if you didn't know how to work the variables you couldn't figure out the equation. He'd grow impatient, and I'd end up feeling hurt and stupid.

I know he didn't mean to make me feel bad, but he did. "I'm sorry," he'd say, "I'm just having a hard time with the mortgage mess. The subprime mortgage pools are a symptom of a much bigger problem."

When I asked him to define a mortgage pool, he'd spout off about collateral, tranches, and risk tolerance, which confused me even more.

After a while, I quit asking; whenever he told me about his business deals, I just listened and nodded.

This seemed like something I should understand, however. So while Wim was unpacking the English shortbread cookies and Royal Guard key chains he'd brought back from London for the kids, I asked, "What does that mean exactly, that the hedge funds have collapsed?"

"It means my business basically shut down," he said.

This news sounded serious, and I wanted to say something helpful, but I bit my tongue, telling myself it was best to avoid irritating him, hopeful that as long as he still had a job and a paycheck, we were okay.

CHAPTER 20: WIM AND THE HOE

Lexington Ave, Rye – June 2007

A s eager as I was to begin the excavation, I was nervous. I couldn't help but think of the story I'd recently heard about a project that had been brought to a standstill when a backhoe driver hit a gas line and it ruptured and exploded. Still, this feeling of jubilation rarely entered our lives anymore—it was generally reserved for bonus time and birthday sex—and now here we were, far from year-end compensation or significant anniversary dates, watching our kids do a tippy-toed happy dance and clap their hands in gleeful anticipation of the big event.

We stood under the blue morning sky, the front yard bustling with a small crew of helmeted demolition workers shouting commands.

"It's really happening," Wim said, putting his arm around my waist and giving my body a half squeeze. I couldn't recall the last time I'd seen him this happy. I glanced at the houses on either side of us—to the left, the Zambonis' large traditional home, distinguished by the Palladian window over its front entry, and to the right, a smaller but quaint brick Cape.

"I'm sure the neighbors are ready too," I said. "How many months has it been?"

"Months?" Wim shook his head. "It's been over a year."

"Hard to believe it's been that long," I said. "But we're going to get exactly what we want."

I imagined coming home to our dream house, pulling into a two-car garage with attached mudroom and entering a space with high ceilings, abundant windows, and oversize closets. The thought made me shudder with joy.

"Farewell, old friend," I said, looking across the dry lawn to the forty-five-year-old house, its dormered roof illuminated by the rising sun. The exterior, a sweet white Cape, was charming in a quiet way. A cluster of English ivy clung to the white brick foundation and trailed upward toward weathered aluminum siding. Green shutters flanked the two bottom windows, which were buffered by an uneven row of boxwoods and azaleas. A patchwork path of red and gray flagstone curved from the driveway to the front door, painted green like the shutters. A modest portico, supported by two narrow aluminum columns, arched over the door. I wondered about the Adamsons, the family that used to live there. What would they think about their house being torn down? Would they be horrified? Would they have done the same thing themselves, given the opportunity?

An excavator nearly as tall as the house roared to life in the driveway.

"Here we go!" I squeezed Wim's hand as the crew began. "Kids, this is it!"

All three of our children stood mesmerized. We winced at the raw screeching of metal against metal as a giant arm flexed forward and steel teeth clamped down onto strips of siding. Shreds of house fell to the ground.

"How long do you think it will take?" I asked.

"I don't know. This is my first demolition." Wim's lips curled up into a broad, dimpled smile, the creases around his sparkling eyes squeezed tight. He readied his Nikon D3, pulling the black camera strap over his head and placing it over the folded collar of his shirt. He peered into the viewfinder and adjusted the lens.

The crew methodically shaved off layers of brick and aluminum siding to segregate recyclable materials; the noise was so deafening, it drowned out the camera's shutter. The driver of the excavator gracefully maneuvered the gigantic claw. He looked like a sculptor scraping away layers of clay.

"There's no going back now." Wim waved his hand toward the shelled house, which, just moments before, had stood under the false protection of centuries-old oak trees. "Take this." He handed me the camera.

"Mom, look!" Paige shouted, tugging at my arm so hard that her curly brown locks bounced around her head like box springs. The claw struck another section of the house, sending debris flying into the air.

I turned to Wim to see his reaction, but he was gone. A few neighbors had wandered outside and gathered to watch the demolition.

"Kids, where did Daddy go?" I shouted, even though everything had fallen silent.

I heard an engine rev. It was hard to make him out through the cloud of testosterone that had formed around his body, but I knew that my husband, who hadn't even driven a stick shift in twenty years, was behind the wheel of the backhoe, his banker's butt straddling the vinyl seat, living out his dual fantasies of operating heavy machinery and pulverizing a house.

That Wim was driving the backhoe didn't come as a complete surprise. Weeks ago, when we were bidding out the demolition, I'd heard him on the phone with one company after another, asking the owners if he could operate the backhoe when the time came. Most of them had just laughed and hung up, but apparently he'd struck a deal with the one he'd ended up hiring. I could picture him working his charms, the phone cradled between his ear and shoulder, sitting in our home office, chair tipped back precariously onto two legs, his feet on the desk, crossed at the ankles, his hands clasped behind his neck. Wim was persuasive; it was something I had always admired about him.

"Why do you want to do this so badly?" I'd asked at the time.

"Doesn't everybody want to knock a house down?" he'd responded.

I knew he saw this as an opportunity to fulfill his need for novelty—the same need that had once gotten him up 2000 feet off the ground in a biplane at an airplane museum in Pennsylvania, and racing 190 miles per hour on the Las Vegas Motor Speedway during a client outing. Whether his thrill-seeking was due to boredom or an addiction to dopamine release, I had no idea. I had long ago learned to stop questioning him.

Until that moment, the only claws Wim had ever maneuvered were the ones belonging to the crane games at the Jersey Shore arcades. Now he was propped before a half dozen control levers and gauges. I pictured his hands compressing the levers and pushing forward. Wim was like a Minotaur—half human, half bull—on the offensive and ready to charge. Confident, competitive, and forceful, the same first-born-child drive that had earned him a profit selling "magic" rocks door-to-door for a quarter each as an eight-year-old boy, and that made him such an effective investment banker as a grown man. His eyes were lit up, his lips set in a grim line of determination. He was empowered; he was a trailblazer; and he was . . . stripping the gears. The mustard-colored machine started bucking up and down in a grinding fury. Wim seemed as if he were battling the vehicle itself instead of the house.

"Is Daddy going to fall over?" Paige asked.

The smell of diesel fuel wafted in the air as the engine droned steadily. Wim finally shifted into gear and propelled the rumbling vehicle forward on its tank-like treads. He clamped down again and this time shifted backward, which triggered a series of backup beeps. I didn't doubt his ability to bulldoze the house as much as I feared him taking down a gas main along with it.

Suddenly, the backhoe barreled ahead and the claw pivoted and came crashing down, taking out half the garage. Wim continued to ram the swing boom wildly into what was left of the garage, kicking storms of dust into the air. The four-person demolition crew shielded their eyes with their sleeves.

In less than a minute, Wim had reduced the two-car garage to smoking rubble. Seemingly having taken his fill of wreckage, he switched the machine off. The landscape grew quiet. My husband came off the digger as wobbly as a cowboy climbing off a bucking bronco.

He made his way across the front yard in his loafers, clumsily stepping down on the giant clumps of earth torn up by the six-ton vehicle. Droplets of sweat were beaded on his forehead. He was shaking.

"Holy shit!" he said. "That was the most exciting thing I've ever done with my clothes on!"

CHAPTER 21: OF UFOS AND PENISES

Lexington Ave, Rye – October 2007

"Let's build a cupola," Luke suggested, the result of our simple request to make our house look original.

"A what?" Wim and I asked.

A cupola, otherwise known as a lantern, turned out to be a dome-like architectural feature used to provide a lookout or to admit light and air. Luke thought it could provide light to the upstairs hallway and give the house character. Wim thought it was a great idea. I was skeptical. So it immediately became a point of contention between us.

"You said you want the house to be unique," Wim said.

"Unique, not bizarre," I said. "I don't want it to look like a UFO landed on top of my house."

"It's a simple ornamental dome. It looks distinct."

"Maybe on a post office," I said. "People will be knocking on our door asking to buy a roll of stamps."

We argued back and forth for days: "It's frivolous"; "It's stylish"; "It's pretentious"; "It's whimsical."

My real problem was that this type of distinction was unheard of in Rye. I was not only worried how the ornament itself would look; I was worried about how it would make *us* look. This was a neighborhood of subdued rooflines. I imagined people walking by our house, pointing and whispering.

But as much comfort and satisfaction as I found in following rules, Wim found even more in challenging them. He and Luke both pushed for the cupola, so eventually I came around.

At least, I said I did. In reality, I couldn't stop worrying about it.

●———●

The day Luke dropped off the front elevations—the architectural drawings showing a vertical perspective, how the front of our house would appear—my heart sank a little.

Wim looked at me. "What's wrong?"

"Nothing," I assured him. I was afraid to bring it up for fear of sending him over the edge.

"Janie, if there's something not right you'd better speak up now, because in a few days they'll be pouring cement."

"It's the roof," I said.

"Really?" He looked surprised. Apparently, I'd done a very good job pretending I liked the idea. "What don't you like about it?"

I hesitated. I couldn't admit that I had a problem with the very feature he'd been a fan of all this time.

"The cupola?"

I nodded.

He scrunched his face in irritation and confusion. "I thought you liked it."

"I do like it; I'm just not convinced that I like it on *our* house."
Wim closed his eyes in that agitated way of his.

"I'm afraid that when it's built, in real life, it won't look right."

"You have to tell Luke," he said. "Soon."

"I'll talk to him," I promised.

•———•

Two days later, Luke and I sat side by side at his drafting table, under a cozy, slanted eave, discussing rooflines. Despite my anxiety, I'd been waiting impatiently all morning to meet with him. Seeing him always gave me a feeling of warmth and energy, like that first sip of coffee in the morning.

Sometimes when I was with Luke I'd find myself thinking back to work relationships I'd had in the past and reflecting on how interesting it is that when you work closely with someone, you sometimes start to have feelings that you question—feelings that you probably shouldn't be feeling.

"I want to understand exactly what concerns you about the cupola," Luke said, transferring his gaze from me to the drawing spread out beneath the octagonal skylight. The bright morning sunlight poured through the window and reflected off the drawing, creating a halo effect around the front elevations that, in my mind, exaggerated the cupola even more. "Of course we can make changes if we need to," he assured me, though he looked horrified.

I stared at the drawing and tried to formulate an intelligent response, but something about sitting this close to him made my breath come up short. "I'm just afraid," I said.

"Don't be," he said. And for the next twenty minutes, he lectured me on residential roof design, throwing around terms like slope, pitch, and vertical proportions. I tried to concentrate on his words but ended up merely staring at his lips.

I loved Luke's patience and his passion, but I was so nervous I almost wanted to stop the project altogether. Perhaps everything was moving too fast and I was trying to slow it down. Perhaps I had cold feet. Maybe I couldn't handle this type of risk.

"It's just so hard for me to imagine," I said.

"What can I do to reassure you?" Luke asked. And then he said, "I have an idea."

•————•

The following Saturday morning, when the three of us were about to convene around our dining room table, Luke was holding something in both hands that I didn't recognize—neither his usual briefcase nor a drawing tube.

He carefully placed a 3-D house model on the table as if it were a royal wedding cake. The model resembled a giant gingerbread house, though it lacked both peppermint candies and gumdrops. "Here's your house," he said, leaning back to admire the small foam-core rendition of our soon-to-be-built home.

I stared at the model, willing it to show me that my fears were unfounded, but all I saw was a bulky box with what looked like an enormous gun turret stuck on top.

Wim popped his eyes at me, as if to say, *Say something*.

"Thank you," I said. But what I wanted to say was, *It's going to look like an alien spacecraft crash-landed on our roof.* I could already hear my new neighbors deleting our names from their holiday party lists.

•————•

"How lovely," Betsy said when I stopped by her office to show her the front elevations of our house a couple of days later.

"What do you think of the cupola?" I asked, surprised that she'd needed prompting.

"I don't think you need it," she said, although she didn't seem appalled by it, as I'd expected she might.

Had I just wanted another opinion? Or had I secretly hoped that conservative Betsy, whose idea of liberal was to wear pants, would not be keen on our bold architectural idea and would provide me with the ammunition to shoot it down?

Later that day, I said to Wim, "I asked Betsy what she thought of the cupola."

"Betsy? She's a real estate agent, not an architect. Why would you ask her?"

I couldn't tell Wim what was churning inside me: A fear that if our cupola looked defective, then I would look defective. That others would judge me as critically as I judged myself.

•———•

After all the back-and-forth about whether to go ahead with it, I finally came to terms with the cupola. And even though it would cost about the price of a used Prius, I'd actually become excited about the idea of being the first in our neighborhood—perhaps the whole town—to have one.

The day the cupola was being framed, I stopped by the house to see how things were progressing. I pulled up past a bevy of construction trucks and parked under the tall oak tree. With my fingers still gripping the steering wheel, I peered through the passenger window and up at the roof of our house. What I felt was not the pride I'd hoped for, however, but dread.

The shaft had been built five feet too tall. Capped with its mushroom-like roof, it looked like a gigantic penis projecting from our rooftop.

How many people had already witnessed this phallic monument protruding from my home? How many people were delighting in my misfortune? One thing I had learned from this project was that when friends and family asked how the house was coming along, they didn't want to hear that things were going well. They wanted unpredictable; they wanted scandalous; they wanted disasters.

I called Wim. "The cupola looks like an oversized penis jutting from our rooftop."

"Penis?"

"Yes!" I said.

"Is this you overreacting? You never like anything at first."

"No, I swear. It doesn't even look like a cupola," I said. "What are we going to do?"

A hundred penis jokes surged through my head, and a part of me wished I could see the humor in our circumstance. I got off the phone, turned to the framer, and barked, "Get that thing off my roof."

●————●

Later that day, I stood at the street with Randy, the site supervisor, our necks craned to watch the roofers dismantle the cupola.

"I agree, Janie. It looked wrong. But we were just following the plans," he said earnestly, his bushy brown mustache pulled down in a frown.

The offending structure was reconfigured as quickly as it had been erected, and by the next day, the dome had shriveled down to half its original size. Now in proportion with the rest of the house, the new and improved cupola looked good, and after all of my hemming and hawing, I was beginning to like it more each day. It was simple. No gun turrets, no UFOs, no three-eyed aliens. Just an elegant lantern adorning our rooftop.

CHAPTER 22: OUT OF BALANCE

Raymond Ave, Rye – October 2007

"What time will you be home tonight?" I asked Wim after spending an afternoon with the contractor talking materials, specs, and timelines, ordering tile, carpooling kids, and feeling like a single parent. I'd had a particularly rough day. Our oldest daughter, Hailey, now twelve, had come home with a fever, compounding my stress. Now I was pressing Wim to come home early.

"I'll be home by eight," he said finally.

Eager for us to share a meal together, I prepared his favorite steak. Eight o'clock rolled around, but there was no familiar sound of the key in the door.

Wim finally called at eight thirty.

"What happened? I've been sitting here waiting for you," I said before he'd had a chance to say hello.

"Sorry, just as I was about to leave the office, Grant called a meeting." He sounded tired, but I couldn't bring myself to empathize, given how much we'd been bickering lately.

I'd wanted so badly to build a house; how could a project that made me feel hopeful and excited also have become such a source of conflict?

"But you said you'd be home by eight. Couldn't you have told him you had to leave?" I said, on the verge of tears.

He breathed loudly through his nose. "Janie, he's my boss. It's not like I can just tell him I have to leave because my wife has a rib-eye resting at home."

His sarcasm only fueled my anger. "You have no idea how hard it is overseeing construction all day and taking care of the kids. Today I didn't even shower."

"Do you think I want to be here? Do you think I want to work until eight, nine o'clock every night? Believe me, I'd much rather be home relaxing on the sofa and spending time with my wife and kids."

I partly believed him. But the way we argued, sometimes I wondered. Sitting in our tiny breakfast nook under our decorative apple plates and looking at the kitchen counter—dirty dishes scattered everywhere—I felt helpless. Exhausted too. I told him so.

"I don't know what you want from me."

"I want your help!"

"I am helping. I'm working hard for us, for our family." He exhaled loudly in one big breath. "I have to go," he said, suddenly, and a second later I heard a dial tone.

Furious, I dialed back, my fingers flying across the buttons on the phone.

"Don't ever hang up on me!" I exploded when he answered.

"I didn't hang up on you."

"Yes you did. That's the rudest thing anyone can ever do!" I screamed. I kept eying the stairway to make sure the kids weren't listening.

"Calm down," he said, words that in any situation are guaranteed to make a person more furious. "Janie, I am at work. I am not going to have this conversation right now. We can discuss it when I get home."

"Fine, bye!" I hung up the phone, threw myself down on the sofa, and sobbed into a cushion. I sat up, grabbed a pair of Wim's underwear from the laundry basket, wadded it up into a ball, and hurled it across the room. "Do your own fucking laundry!" I shouted at the white cotton boxer briefs that I had bought him on sale at Macy's the week before. They floated through the air and grazed the ceiling fan before landing a woefully short distance away, making me feel even more helpless than I already did.

Staring at the ceiling, I watched the fan blades rotate until they slowed to a stop. The fan reminded me of our marriage: two independent sets of blades operating as one unit, blades that sometimes fell out of balance and caused the fan to wobble. The fan, I knew, could usually be fixed with a little extra care. I also knew that in some cases, if you let the fan wobble for too long, you'll have to rebuild it altogether.

CHAPTER 23: MY LITTLE BLACK BOOK

Raymond Ave, Rye – October 2007

Over the following months, Luke and I spent a lot of time together. During school hours, whenever I wasn't driving through neighborhoods photographing inspiring homes and poring over home magazines, I was with our architect.

Other than Wim, this was the most time I'd spent with any man since college, and it felt strange. I'd been a stay-at-home mom for twelve years. The only time I was around men anymore was at the occasional cocktail party, and even then I mostly chatted with women. On the rare occasion when I came into contact with a middle-aged man, he was either delivering my FedEx package, shmearing my bagel with cream cheese, or striding past my house from the train station, carrying the burden of his mortgage in his briefcase. Since marrying Wim, the closest encounter I'd had with another man was with my dentist, and even he saw me as just a mouth; I'd only been intimate with his appliances.

Sitting at my dining room table one morning, just the two of us, surrounded by rolls of blueprints, Luke and I discussed design details. I had in my possession the Black Book. Not the proverbial little black book from my single life; gone were the days that I needed a relationship tool to catalogue the phone numbers, addresses, and secrets of lovers and ex-lovers. I had entered a new passage in my life in which data had replaced dating, tray ceilings had replaced ashtrays, and semi-gloss had replaced lip gloss.

My Black Book, the one that had grown so large I'd had to create a separate kitchen binder, was a three-inch round-ring vinyl binder, organized room by room, that contained inspirational cutouts of magazine photos and Polaroids of design elements I wanted to incorporate in our home. It was thicker than a dictionary and longer than *Moby Dick*, and it already had so much wear I'd had to repair the page holes with hole-punch reinforcements and bind the broken spine with special tape the way my grandma used to do at my school library. I leaned on it like a friend. I carried it like a baby. And I referred to it as if it were the Holy Bible.

Still, regardless of what kind of book it was, I'd never spent this many hours with a man and not had sex. I was suddenly aware of how we were relating, conscious of what felt to me like a good vibe. Building this house had stirred something inside of me, maybe something a little bit dangerous.

"What do you want the front door to look like?" Luke asked.

"This," I said, flipping through the 'Facade' section of my binder until I reached the *Renovation Style* photo of a shingle-style home with a beautiful mahogany door surrounded by art deco leaded glass. "I like using pictures," I explained.

Luke glanced at the binder and nodded. "It's helpful."

I smiled, pleased to have my efforts recognized.

"The door will be custom made, and I have glass samples I can show you," he said. "How about your family room fireplace mantle? Any ideas?"

I turned to the fireplace section and pointed to a classic limestone mantle featured in *Architectural Digest*. "What do you think?"

"That will look great," he said.

Though I'd become more familiar with Luke, in some ways I'd become less at ease, with increased awareness of how close I was sitting to him, whether I had lipstick on my teeth, and whether I needed to pop another Tic Tac.

"Any other special features you'd like in the family room?"

I turned back a few pages and showed him several photos of built-in window seats. "Can you custom design it to look like these, but make it an oversize daybed that fits a twin bed?"

"A bed?"

"Our friends in Texas have one. They made it deep enough to fit a mattress and custom upholstered it. It's a great cozying-up space. It has built-in storage underneath for games and photo albums." I envisioned myself snuggling with my kids in the window seat and playing Crazy Eights on a snowy day.

Luke had an amused twinkle in his eye. "Yes, we can do that."

Once we were done with the family room, he explained that our kitchen designer would take care of details like cabinet dividers for cookie sheets and locating appliances. He handed me a list of cabinetmakers he'd worked with, and as I reached forward, my hand accidentally brushed against his. I felt a quiver but pretended not to notice. Nothing registered on his face.

"Moving on to the second floor. Let's talk about your and Wim's bedroom," he said.

My face and ears grew hot. Suddenly, it wasn't the kids I was picturing myself snuggling with.

CHAPTER 24: DOUBLE FUDGE SUNDAE

Raymond Ave, Rye – October 2007

"Home theaters are over-the-top," I said one night, trying to steer Wim away from something I considered an unnecessary extravagance. Aside from the cost, I hated the idea of everyone sitting in his or her own chair watching movies together but separately. Wasn't family movie time supposed to be spent watching *and* cuddling?

Wim and I worked toward a shared vision for our dream house until it came to the basement. He wanted a home theater, with leather cinema-style seating and a sixty-inch TV, where he could watch *Die Hard* and hear the explosions in surround sound. I argued that the seats would interfere with the game tables I would be using to entertain my girlfriends during Friday-night bunko, a dice game we used as an excuse for social drinking and jokingly referred to as "drunko."

"Our entire project is over-the-top," Wim said. "We're not building a cabin in the woods. Did you see the latest construction invoice?"

No, in fact, I hadn't seen the invoice; paying the bills was Wim's job. Over the years, we'd taken turns paying bills, until one day I'd accidentally withdrawn instead of deposited money from our checking account and caused dozens of checks to bounce. Now it was my job to open the mail. And whenever I opened an invoice from the construction company, I shielded my eyes from the numbers. I knew how much things cost; I just didn't want to know what they added up to. I wasn't proud of my ostrich-like behavior, but I couldn't help myself.

I figured Wim would let me know if we'd spent too much, the same way he sometimes did when our Visa bill came due. "We have to cut back," he'd say. Reminding him of last year's bonus never helped. The notion of a bonus was a tricky one in his business. In its crudest form, it was a little like being a waiter. There was a base salary, but it wasn't at all commensurate with what his job entailed. The bonus was like pulling tips; it was the money we largely lived off of.

Our standard of living had always been defined by Wim's bonuses—and for years, those bonuses had been ample. But they were never guaranteed. No matter how big his bonus was in any given year, he always had to worry about the next one.

In deference to his concerns, at the beginning of each fiscal year, we always made a conscious effort to eat out less often and turn off the lights when we left the room. Then, a few weeks later, we'd return to our normal habits.

The truth is, I was happy to allow Wim to be the one in charge. I was essentially like a child. I didn't pay bills, I didn't know how much things amounted to, and I blithely assumed everything would be okay.

We didn't realize while building the house how temptation can trick you into confusing need with desire. It's like being firmly committed to your diet, then being tempted by a double fudge sundae. How easy it is to say, "We'll just splurge on a Sub-Zero refrigerator for the kitchen. After all, we're only doing this once." But it all adds up, and pretty soon you've left Jenny Craig for Ben & Jerry. And then, of course, you spring for the Sub-Zero freezer.

Sitting on the sofa beside me, Wim had a coffee table book propped on his lap to support the drawing he had sketched of two game rooms in the basement adjoined by oversize double sliding doors. "We can put a pool table in this room and a Ping-Pong table and a few arcade games in the other." He looked hungrily at the entertainment space that we imagined filling with friends and family, young and old. I wondered if it reminded him of being a teenager in Upstate New York, spending long winters hanging out in a basement filled with beanbag chairs, a Ping-Pong table, and his sister's balance beam. I didn't share those kinds of sub-terranean memories. Like many native Californians, I was raised in a house built on a concrete slab and only knew how to relax above ground. But this wasn't my playhouse with my rules. We were doing this together.

In our old house, we'd wanted a Ping-Pong table but hadn't been able to find a spot for it. At one point we'd considered putting one in the dining room, but even that room had been too small. Our new home would have a basement that spanned the entire length of the house—enough space for three Ping-Pong tables and a pool table to boot.

But now, even two thousand square feet weren't enough to satisfy Wim. It wasn't enough that we could fit an entire Peruvian village in our rec room, or that we would soon have a guest suite with enough amenities—including a king-size bed and wall TV—to run a bed and breakfast, complete with white fluffy towels and a soaking tub. It wasn't enough that we had a playroom *and* a billiards room.

"I like the idea of multiple game rooms," I said. I gave his arm a squeeze, and he looked up and smiled. I loved seeing him excited about our house and planning how to maximize the fun we'd have in it. It made me feel like my own ongoing spending frenzy was okay.

A few months earlier, Wim had decided he wanted to take advantage of the opportunity to add additional square footage. He said it was for resale value. We'd gone through the same debate over yard size when we were house hunting. I'd have settled for enough space for a barbecue, whereas Wim wanted a backyard park. "I want land," he said. I reminded him that we weren't raising cattle.

If he couldn't possess the whole North American continent, he'd decided, he could at least dig under the garage and create an all-purpose room in the basement.

"We'll have so much space down there; why do we need to dig more?" I'd asked.

"Because we can. Space is at a premium in this town. It will create value."

It all made sense. Wim always made sense.

"What about safety?" I asked. "I don't want my minivan crashing through the ceiling."

"We'll install steel beams for support, like they do in a parking garage."

"This isn't Port Authority," I said.

He shut his eyes for a moment, as if gathering patience. "You've made decisions on the kitchen, family room, master bathroom . . . can I at least have a say on a room *under* our house?"

I nodded, reminding myself that I'd recently decided, against Wim's better judgment, to hire our expensive kitchen designer,

Joan, to also design our master bathroom, and that I should take his needs into consideration. Besides, he was the one with good business sense. A great deal of energy and money was flowing out the door with this project, but I trusted that he wouldn't allow all of it to run out.

CHAPTER 25: SCONES AND SCONCES

Raymond Ave, Rye – October 2007

As the process continued, we were forced to make more decisions that seemed impossibly premature. It felt to me as if the foundation had barely been poured when Glenn—our operations manager, the guy whose job it was to coordinate the building aspect of the project—began bombarding me with emails: *What type of hardware are you using? How tall do you want your bathroom vanity? Where do you want your shower niche?* As he explained that things like tile required a long lead time, he warned, "You need to stay on top of the construction schedule I gave you. You're going to have an entire house's worth of decisions to make before it's all over."

If it had been difficult for me to visualize the house plans, it was even harder for me to imagine how everything would eventually all come together. Like making a paper snowflake, you snip here and you snip there, but you don't know what it's really going to look like until you open it up for the reveal, and it would be a long while until we opened our snowflake.

The project cycled in waves of intensity, which for me brought on waves of obsession. We were finally enjoying a lull in decision-making while the roof was going up, and then—bam! Floors were upon us. I started researching flooring on the Internet and learning everything there was on the subject—tile, concrete, wood, stone—just to satisfy myself that what we were selecting was the best choice for us. I was plagued by my own compulsive need to know that I had researched every possible option; only then, I felt, could I make the "right" decision. Usually, "right" meant I found a product identical to the magazine picture I'd pasted into my Black Book—or, in the rare case that I didn't have a picture, a product that matched the vision I had in my head.

I wanted perfection. I wanted every floor, window, and hinge to look perfect, operate perfectly, and coordinate perfectly. My self-worth depended on it. For years I had listened to my dad tell me how my mom had worked tirelessly with their architect to design a perfect house. I'd grown up feeling like I needed to live up to those expectations. My parents had raised me to have high standards, and it had imbued me with a strong need to control every aspect of my life, especially how others perceived me. This was my opportunity to achieve a level of perfectionism that would make me feel worthy and accepted.

•———•

Time forced us to divvy up much of the decision-making responsibility. Wim and I divided tasks by giving each other "honeydew" lists, the catchy little phrase meaning, "Honey, do this," and "Honey, do that"—or, more accurately, "Please do all the tedious crap I don't want to do." I was anointed Queen of Color, charged with overseeing everything related to hue and design. Even things as mundane as door hinges. Wim was relegated to anything I found even more boring than hinges, like fireplaces, insulation, and stereo systems.

Wim and I habitually debriefed one another on each day's progress by phone or email. *What did the plumber say about the mudroom faucet? Do we have an estimate for the exterior stone? What type of windows should we order?* I liked working as a team—solving construction problems together, bonding over plumbing and electrical.

We spent one evening huddled in front of our computer in our home office, researching energy-efficient windows. Sitting there beside my husband, I recalled our early years together, when we'd been forced to make tough decisions about whether and how to continue our long-distance relationship. Now we were making decisions on double- versus triple-pane windows.

As I studied *Consumer Reports* window-buying tips on the computer and Wim foraged in the fridge for a snack, an email from Luke arrived in my inbox. My heart skipped a beat as I read his message.

In my last email about light fixtures, I had inadvertently omitted the letter "c," typing *scones* instead of *sconces*. Luke had just replied, *Do you want jelly on your scones, and how do you take your tea?*

In the previous couple of months, our emails had become less formal and more playful. Typos had become our own little in-joke. It was fun to flirt in a way that I hadn't in a long time. It was a thrill to detect an interest aimed in both directions. The connection between us left me feeling giddy.

I was smiling, trying to think of a clever comeback, when Wim entered the room holding a red apple. I scrambled to turn off my email, then asked myself why. *It's just an innocent email*, I reminded myself. But if I thought it might make Wim uncomfortable, did that make it wrong? I had to admit, I was getting emotional satisfaction from my relationship with Luke. I loved Wim, but our marriage had become so routine it was like a restaurant menu that never changed. I wasn't looking to make a complete overhaul—just to spice things up a little.

"Luke asked about sconces," I told Wim, ready to refocus on lighting.

•———•

Luke's design philosophy, "less is more," had become our golden rule. He often recited this mantra whenever we were stymied over a design decision, and we'd obey, trusting his inclination toward keeping things simple.

Still, I often felt overwhelmed, so much so that my anxiety was beginning to play out in my dreams. "Even in my dream last night, Luke couldn't help me make a decision," I told Wim one morning.

"You dreamt about Luke?" Wim frowned.

"Yes," I said. "We were preparing a dinner party with him. We all planned the menu together but couldn't decide on the entrée. We finally narrowed it down to bouillabaisse or chili. Then we settled on chili but debated over how to make a perfect chili. We scoured stacks of cookbooks in search of the perfect recipe, but we couldn't agree on one. I told Luke, 'How about we give this one a try?' But he said, 'Too many pinto beans. Remember, less is more!'"

I didn't tell Wim about the last part of the dream: "How about this one?" I'd asked. "Not spicy enough," Dream-Luke had said, and I thought I'd caught a naughty gleam in his eye. One that turned me on.

"So what happened?" Wim was asking.

"We never found the perfect recipe."

Wim blinked, not sure what to make of me.

•————•

I knew our project would be challenging, but I honestly hadn't expected building a house to be such a big undertaking. Even with an overinvolved architect, a kitchen and bathroom designer, and an interior designer, it was a full-time job. However, this was not something I often shared out loud. I was aware that it was a full-time *spending* job and not a full-time *earning* job. Instead, I talked to Wim about progress.

He said things like, "Things are moving fast now. The framing especially."

And I agreed: "Yes, the frame has gone up so quickly."

Our dream house was suddenly like a maze of timber. Soon, the house would be wrapped in Tyvek paper, the protective cover that later would come to insulate Wim and me in an entirely different way. Assuming we lasted that long.

CHAPTER 26: ALMOST AROUSING

Raymond Ave, Rye – October 2007

L ately, things were seeming bleak. Even our Jewish New Year celebration two weeks earlier at our friends Sharon and Brian Sadowski's house hadn't held its usual festive vibe. The adults, rattled by the fall of housing prices, had chattered through Rosh Hashanah dinner about plummeting asset values while the children talked among themselves at the other end of the table. The apples and honey on the table, symbolic of a sweet New Year, contradicted the worrisome conversation.

Every year it was the same. Same rituals. Same friends. Only this year it felt different. It was fall of 2007, and there was a feeling of doom in the air. I sat quietly in the middle of it all, sipping my wine, staring from one adult to the other—each with a background in finance—listening to them debate the financial market and Bear Stearns hedge funds imploding and wishing I understood what they were talking about. I had scanned the headlines, tried to understand the stories . . . Sub-prime loans were taking a lot of funds down and were eliminating people's jobs along the way. Wim was knee-deep in this, so his job, and our livelihood, was acutely at risk. That much I got.

Outside, the leaves were turning rust and gold. There were dozens of pumpkins growing on thick vines in the corner of the Sadowskis' yard. Had I decided on the crown molding yet? I couldn't remember.

"So, Wim, is this a crisis or isn't it?" Sharon was asking him.

I noticed the heavy creases on Wim's forehead, the weight of apprehension in the room. Still, I couldn't help looking around Sharon and Brian's spacious dining room and imagining us hosting Rosh Hashanah dinner at our new house next year, at our own dining room table, which I would finally be able to extend with both leaves to accommodate fifteen dinner guests.

"That's the million-dollar question," Brian interjected. Brian had recently retired from his job in finance, news that had made Wim envious when Brian had first made the announcement. "He's almost ten years older than you," I'd reminded Wim, hoping that would make him feel better. But it hadn't.

Brian and Wim were discussing bankruptcy protection when another couple, the Bensons, broke in. As they took over, I caught Wim's subtle nod, a signal that he was ready to leave.

On the drive home, I said, "What was everyone talking about?"

"The financial market is in turmoil," he said with a wary voice. He was fiddling with his wedding ring, continuously spinning it with his thumb as he steered the car. It unnerved me, the thought that he was nervous.

"Do you think—"

"I can't talk about it anymore tonight," he interrupted, an edge to his voice. Maybe he noticed the hurt look on my face, because he softened and said, "We can discuss it another time." Then he fell silent, and he remained so for the rest of the drive.

•———•

Despite the seriously bad news affecting the stock market, economy, and Wim's job, I was still shopping. Designing the house had been the hard part—now I got to do the fun part, furnishing it. I spent hours shopping for just the right thing, enraptured by the beauty and functionality of each piece.

One October morning, after I'd dropped the kids off at school, I boarded the Metro-North Railroad from Rye to Manhattan with my interior designer, Faye. She was taking me to the famous Decoration and Design Building (a.k.a. the D&D Building), where, as a certified interior designer, she had official access to it all: Scalamandré silks, Grange furniture, and Osborne & Little wallpapers.

Dressed for the occasion in linen slacks and a sleeveless cotton blouse, I tugged gently at the strand of pearls around my neck, bouncing lightly on my seat, anxious and excited to explore this goldmine of designer furnishings and accessories, where I would finally take my books of inspirational interiors from fantasy to reality and find special things that no one else was going to have. The conductor called out stations over the loudspeaker—"New Rochelle, New Rochelle! Next stop, New Rochelle!"—as New York whipped by. I took note of the vinyl seats, a sea of drab brown; not even train upholstery escaped my notice these days.

Thirty minutes later, we were weaving through the Upper East Side in a taxicab. As we approached Third Avenue and passed Bloomingdale's—their flagship store—my palms began to sweat, my heart beat violently, and my cheeks flushed crimson. I could hardly contain my excitement.

The cab driver pulled up in front of a gray stone high-rise; I threw a small wad of bills in his direction and ran for the entrance. Faye was one step ahead of me.

She strained against the massive steel-gauge designer doors with all ninety-nine pounds of her body weight, and we entered.

I stood, awestruck, taking it all in, frozen like one of the statues in the lobby, marveling at the impressive vaulted, coffered ceiling and the divine white Carrera marble floors and walls, which resembled beautiful cumulus clouds and were radiant in the glow of the soft lighting. I felt as if I had just entered the pearly gates of heaven. Shopping for and thinking about the house made me giddy and light—a stark contrast to Rosh Hashanah dinner, where I'd been tipsy with wine yet sobered by the conversation.

Faye turned to me. "Are you ready?"

"Sure," I said, forcing a yawn to mask my tears of joy.

"Let's go." Faye strode forward with the confidence of a Westminster show dog while I followed behind with the eagerness of a gamboling lamb.

We boarded the elevator. At the eighteenth floor, the doors opened upon a long hallway studded with endless rows of design stores. I feasted my eyes on colorful oriental rugs, expressive textiles in shimmering metallics, and exotic wall-coverings in cork, silk, and fabric. It was an intoxicating cornucopia of beautiful things—and I had access to it all!

Faye led me first to Kravet, where an array of food was sumptuously displayed on a chintz tablecloth: crustless watercress sandwiches, poppy seed bagels, miniature muffins, and raspberry jam. We stopped for a quick nibble and a steaming double cappuccino.

"Can I help you, ladies?" asked a saleswoman dressed head to toe in Gucci, not a section of blouse untucked or a hair out of place. I wondered if that was her Chihuahua wearing the fur stole and diamond-studded collar and staring me down from its perch on a velvet sofa, its eyes saying, *Hands off, señora, this sofa belongs to me.*

"Thank you, we're fine," said Faye.

Sitting at a café table, sipping my gourmet coffee, the moment, steeped in gracious, relaxed living, seemed to capture everything I was feeling. This was the life of my dreams—albeit in a showroom.

We entered Donghia and passed the silks and the linens, hesitated briefly at the cottons, then settled at the forgiving chenilles, where we waded through hundreds of swatches, each neatly hung on its own hanger. I was drawn to the neutrals and soon found myself knee-deep in beige. I wasn't one of those people who needed to see a color consultant to help them go un-beige or find their inner fuchsia. I wasn't afraid of color; I was sick of it. Every room in my old house was a different jewel tone, and I was ready to give bold color a rest.

"Now, I know you want neutrals, but given that you have three kids, we don't want to go too light." Faye rifled through fabric swatches faster than a bank teller counting out bills.

"Right," I said. There was a sample of ice blue velvet hanging beside me. I reached out and stroked it, unable to resist the sensuality of its smooth surface, soft and fleshy under my fingertips. It was almost arousing.

As I fondled the fabric, it struck me that neither of us really knew my price range. Faye had asked for our budget on more than one occasion, but I'd never given her a straight answer. The truth was, I wasn't sure. I only knew I had a vision, and I planned to execute it.

When Wim had suggested that I create an interior design budget for each room, I'd told him it was too hard. "I have no idea what it costs to furnish and decorate an entire house," I'd said with a shrug. So we'd come up with a lump sum instead, a ballpark figure equivalent to the cost of the new car I wouldn't be buying. Hailey, already expressing enthusiasm about getting her driver's license in a few years, would have to resign herself to the fate of sharing my minivan. At the rate we were blowing through our savings on the house, she was lucky her college funds were safely tucked away in untouchable savings accounts.

Eventually, Faye would figure out that we wanted the best mid-price furniture and upholstery she could find. Initially, I had run every invoice Faye gave me for sofas, chairs, and rugs past Wim for his approval. But ever since a recent argument—"Why can't you just take care of things without me?"—it had been up to me to decide, and I was often confused. Wim had given me free range to spend what I wanted, but it was disorienting to shop without a budget.

There was a voice inside my head that dared me to go ahead and dive into the sumptuous embroideries and jacquards, to give in to silks and linens. To go for broke and ignore price tags. To blow everything on luxurious velvet window seats with coordinating custom pillows and draperies, and bedrooms with tufted upholstered headboards and matching fine silk curtains with decorative tassels.

Meanwhile, Faye placed a hand on my arm and repeated the words I didn't seem to have access to: "That fabric is out of your price range."

Yes, my decorator was the one urging me to be more practical. We moved on.

CHAPTER 27: LOOKING FOR MR. POTATO HEAD

Rosemead, CA – September 1992

"What the . . . ?" Wim stopped and cocked his head. It was a hot Saturday night in September. My husband and I had been getting frisky in our bedroom, and we'd just felt a rhythmic vibration that wasn't our own.

"It's coming from next door," I whispered. "Again."

"Why are you whispering?" Wim whispered back. "Are you afraid you'll distract her?"

I gave him a swat on the shoulder. The series of grunts and yelps penetrating the wall suggested that Judy was engaging in fierce sex with howler monkeys. A gruff and greasy-haired bus driver, Judy liked to entertain guests in her apartment—boyfriends, passengers, zoo animals, I couldn't be sure. But judging by the force with which her bed pounded against the wall at all hours of the night, *someone* was driving Judy's bus, and she liked it.

"My God, it sounds like she's having sex wars with another couple in there," I said.

"Either that or she has rechargeable batteries."

A loud moan reverberated through our bedroom.

"That's enough to crush a man's sex drive," Wim said, rolling off me in frustration, his face and shoulders silhouetted against the dim light escaping from the hallway. "Will it ever stop?"

Finally, the noise subsided. I pulled our yellow floral Laura Ashley comforter up to my chest.

"I think it's over," I said, reaching for my water glass on the night table. "Or not." I sighed as we heard the bed squeaking and bumping against the wall.

Wim snorted. "And we were so worried about the train noise when we moved in." He got out of bed, stepped into his crumpled boxer shorts, and left the bedroom. A few minutes later, he returned with a golf club and started banging on the wall with the handle. We heard cackling, followed by more pounding. Wim banged the wall some more.

Before long, Wim and Judy had a cross-beat going; his three beats against her two created what sounded like an African call-and-response prayer, one that I feared might anger the apartment gods.

The pounding subsided. Then, a few minutes later, *Thump! Thump!*

Wim faced the wall and put his hands up in surrender. "I give up," he said, pulling on a T-shirt and a pair of sweatpants. He turned on *The Late Show with David Letterman* and turned up the volume. I knew we were both thinking the same thing: *Get me out of here.*

Normally, when tenant problems arise, one tenant takes things up with management. But our landlords were my parents. How could we complain about anything when they were letting us live there rent-free?

Seeking to invest in something beyond their children's educations, my parents had purchased this small, twenty-unit multi-family dwelling—a pale stucco flat-roofed apartment building on a quiet cul-de-sac dotted with palm trees—in Rosemead, California. Rosemead is a small city, which by LA standards means 50,000 people, or the daily number of visitors to Disneyland. Located about twenty miles east of downtown Los Angeles, it's not far from Downey, where I grew up, but is half the size.

My parents generously footed the bill while Wim and I attended graduate school in the hopes that helping us further our educations would propel us into successful careers. In their minds, a graduate education was more an expectation than a hope. They believed in the value of education as a path to opportunity for themselves and their children. By the time I completed my master's program in social work—my second go-round in graduate school—I had spent more time collecting degrees than earning a paycheck. Still, my parents asked, "How about a PhD?"

Over the course of our three years living in Rosemead, Wim and I both attended the University of Southern California. However, our classes were on opposite ends of campus and were taught, from my perspective, through the lenses of opposing social ideals. Wim's MBA program, based largely on free market competition, would prepare him to take on the world. My MSW would prepare me to worry about it.

Rosemead is an ethnically diverse city similar to my hometown of Downey, with a large Hispanic population and a mix of blue- and white-collar workers. Wim and I lived in an area that was a mix of apartment buildings and small homes, and we would often take walks in the "nice neighborhood," where big houses were set back on expansive green lawns. During our early months there— before Wim's mood began to sour—we often strolled hand in hand along the sidewalk past the mansionettes and dreamed aloud.

"Would you rather live in this house?" I'd point to an English Tudor with a steeply pitched roofline and stained glass windows. "Or that one?" I'd nod to a beautiful Spanish-style home with a clay tile roof shaded by tangerine trees and a stone walkway lined with rose bushes.

"Which one has lower taxes?" he'd say.

As if creating the Mr. Potato Head of our youths, we would pick out the best features of one house and combine them with the best features of another to create our own perfect vision—our fantasy home. Preferably it would not be in Rosemead but a place where we could walk to restaurants, shop at farmers markets, and enjoy Sunday barbecues with neighbors.

Then we'd go back to our pint-size apartment and listen to Judy and her partner thump like jackrabbits.

CHAPTER 28: TOMMY

Lexington Ave, Rye – January 2008

When I drove up to the house and opened the front door to check on the morning progress, I wasn't prepared for what I encountered.

I'd developed a knack for knowing who I would find on site before I'd even stepped across the threshold. If the company logos painted on the sides of the trucks parked outside our house didn't clue me in, the music playing from the old, paint-splashed boom box plugged into a generator by the long extension cord that hung down from the second to first floor was a dead giveaway. I often entered the house against a forceful blast of music that echoed down from upstairs, a flurry of sounds exploding from the crackling speaker.

If the painters were working, the music was Latin American, frenzied and wild. When I walked through my new front door, I entered a soulful world of painting troubadours who sung lyrics aloud to the background of lively guitar strumming in a way that made me want to whip up my skirt and dance the flamenco.

The lively beat made me nostalgic for Los Angeles and standing in my friend Marlena's kitchen, listening to salsa music while helping her grandma make Christmas tamales wrapped in corn husks and tied with twine. It surprised me how much I'd missed Latino culture since our move to Rye. Even though I hadn't broken a piñata since I was ten or road-tripped to Tijuana since my late teens or spoken Spanish with coworkers in years, I still yearned for the culture I'd grown up with—the people, ideas, and customs. Though Rye was a great town, everyone came from the same stock—same race, ethnicity, and religious values. Everyone was white and Christian. Only a few Jews lived in Rye, and I was related to most of them. When we'd first bought our Raymond Avenue house, we'd discovered that Jews in Rye were outnumbered by Tibetan terriers. To help friends navigate their way to our annual Hanukkah party, I learned to say, "Look for the house without the Christmas lights."

But on this morning, it wasn't music that greeted me as I stepped inside. In the middle of the foyer stood a big black mutt—wagging his tail, panting, and staring up at me as if he wondered what I was doing there. I looked around the frat house–like surroundings: a mess of discarded pizza boxes, soda cans, and water bottles were strewn about the house. I looked down the hallway into the kitchen: an array of subcontractors—painters, carpenters, and tile installers—were belching, cursing, and poking fun at each other. Nothing seemed out of the ordinary.

To my left, carpenters had stationed their sawhorse in the middle of the living room and were applying casing to the living room windows. To my right, boxes filled with toilets and bathroom hardware dotted our congested dining room, which was serving as a temporary warehouse for vanities, faucets, and appliances awaiting their final inspection and subsequent assignment to their designated bathrooms. Boxes of cabinetry as big as coffins sat in the kitchen, unopened, waiting for installation day.

"Hello?" I called out, to no one in particular. "Does this dog belong to anyone?"

My eyes scanned the foyer and then the stairway leading up to the second-floor landing, where they settled on what could only be described as a statue of David—a splendid form reflecting the bright sunlight that glanced in from the cupola above and gave the room a warm, sensuous glow. I took in the finely shaped body, chiseled jawline, and mane of thick hair.

David bounded down the stairs two at a time. We looked at each other for a short moment, and the next thing I knew he was holding me, pulling me in close while together we launched into synchronized motion, dancing cheek to cheek in perfect step across the foyer to the rhythm of two hearts beating as one. I anticipated his dip and locked my leg around his, leaned my body against his chiseled abs as he dropped me low and swayed me in a smooth circle before returning me to an upright position.

In reality, he detached a dangling cigarette butt from his lips and offered his hand. "Hi, I'm Tommy," he said. His skin was not smooth and pale like marble. His hand was rough and his face was tan, with the perfect hint of five o'clock shadow. He wore a fitted T-shirt and jeans, and a leather bag hung off his construction-worker hip.

I stumbled over my words and my feet as I reached to accept his manly grip. "Nice," I said. "Hi to meet you. I mean, nice to meet you."

Why did I feel like a nervous teenager standing before this man nearly twenty years my junior? So what if he looked like a younger version of Daniel Day-Lewis—tall and lean, thick dark hair, dreamy brown eyes outlined by thick eyebrows and a broad chest I longed to snuggle against?

Tommy cleared his throat. He told me he was there to install our permanent stairway. "This," he held a palm out, "is Shadow, my dog and work partner." He gave me a wink, and I felt my heart race as if he'd just proposed. My God, what was happening to me?

It was strange to have a man who wasn't the scruffy old guy behind the deli counter at Stop & Shop wink at me. I'd been living in a safe world of moms and kids for over a decade now; I was unprepared to suddenly be dealing with men. Handsome, well-built, charming men. Which begged two questions: Why were guys who work construction always so good-looking? And why were they so deft at flirting? I didn't know, exactly. What I did know was that it excited me.

I noticed a leash trailing from Shadow's collar to a work truck parked out front. I reached out tentatively and brushed the hairy beast with my fingertips. A mass of coarse black hair unleashed itself with tornado-like fury onto my white pants, landing in thick layers. Ordinarily, this would have sent me into a frantic twenty-yard dash to the closest lint roller. But I just smiled sweetly.

"The baby deer is still in the front yard," Tommy said.

I repeated his words silently, looking for clues, but found none. I thought his message might be code for "I want you desperately."

When I didn't respond, he tried again. "There's a very young fawn curled up under the mulberry bush out front, and it's been lying there by itself all morning."

My heart skipped a beat. Was there anything more appealing than a man feeling protective of a helpless animal?

A minute later, I was staring down at a fawn that lay all alone in the shrubs, camouflaged by the underbrush, looking very out of place behind the port-a-john. It looked scared. I tried to remind myself that deer always looked scared. I nudged my mind back to the words Tommy had just spoken.

Deer. Yard.

Yard. Dear.

Was Tommy trying to seduce me?

CHAPTER 29: MEETING BEHIND CLOSED DOORS

Lexington Ave, Rye – January 2008

I hadn't been to the house since drywalling had begun the previous week, and there was Sheetrock and plaster dust everywhere.
I started coughing as soon as I entered. The subcontractors worked
through it without masks, as if the thick clouds of chalky dust were
merely a figment of my imagination.

Through the dusty haze I spotted Vince, the new site supervisor, who stood passively in the living room, leaning against
the wall.

Somewhere along the line, Vince had replaced Randy, who
had stopped showing up to work. That's when I'd learned that a
new home is constructed in stages, with different construction
supervisors overseeing each stage. It made me sad that after months
of working with Randy, asking and answering myriad questions,
mediating arguments, and circumcising cupolas together, I'd never
had a chance to say goodbye.

The end of our relationship harkened back to the feelings of separation anxiety I'd long struggled with—feelings that, over the years, I'd learned were about loss of connectedness. "Abandonment represents a core human fear," my therapist, Linda, had once explained. "We've all experienced it." Feeling this now, I was reminded of how I could be surrounded by people, even friends and family, and still be lonely.

I gave Vince a slight wave and walked toward him. Unlike the builder, Brodie, whose gruff and direct manner had always intimidated me, Vince was quiet and shy. Doe-eyed and round in the middle, he resembled a stuffed bear and seemed as harmless as one.

"We need you to make a decision on the hardware for the French doors," he said without looking at me as I approached. I noticed that his face was covered in stubbly growth and his wavy brown hair was in need of a trim.

"I know," I said, adjusting the unwieldy stack of binders that was weighing down my arms. Choosing door hardware throughout the house had been challenging because every decision was loaded with nuances. Did I want passage handles or handles that locked? Did I want the finish to match the bedroom on one side of the handle and the connecting bathroom on the other? Were levers really the best way to go?

I was about to refer to my inspiration photos one last time when Luke rounded the corner. "Watch out, Vince, here comes trouble," he said with a chuckle, playfully shielding himself from me.

I flashed him a look but smiled inwardly, secretly reveling in the attention. Vince looked uncomfortable.

Luke smiled at me. "I'm glad you're here. I have a list of questions for you."

"First we need to finish up with the hardware," Vince said, still without making eye contact, as if being in our presence were unpleasantly intimate. "Do you want the handles on the French doors to match the ones we installed on the other doors?"

I looked at Luke uneasily. He loved egg-shaped knobs, and I knew he had been disappointed when I'd decided on using levers throughout the house. Though I shared his appreciation of classic architecture, I knew that levers were the easiest, most comfortable way to open a door. With just one finger, or an elbow or hip, I could push open my door without having to set down my groceries or, someday, my cane. Now, with only the French doors remaining, I was tempted to choose egg knobs just to please Luke. But I didn't.

"Yes," I said, feeling like a traitor. "Levers, please."

"That's fine," Luke said.

Vince moved on to supervise the drywall laborers, leaving Luke and me alone in the living room. It was an unseasonably warm day, and I noticed Luke was wearing shorts and leather flip-flops; the outfit made him look so much more relaxed than he had the first time we'd met, when he'd shown up in a suit and tie. I wondered at what point things had grown so casual that shorts had replaced suits, short sleeves had replaced long, and sandals had replaced Oxfords. Probably around the time that "Hi" had replaced "Dear Wim and Janie" in email greetings.

Despite Luke's continuing to refer to himself by his first and last name in phone messages, there was no doubt that our relationship had grown increasingly familiar and comfortable over the last few months.

"Are those anti-preppy shorts?" I said, nodding toward Luke's Bermuda shorts, which were speckled with embroidered skulls and crossbones, a clear deviation from the polo players adorning most men's shorts in Rye.

"Aye." He grinned mischievously. Luke didn't fit the typical Rye profile: married, two kids, living in an expensive house and wintering in Naples and summering at the Cape. He had a wife but no children, lived in a modest home in a nearby rural suburb, and was just starting out as an independent architect.

"Nice." I smiled. The first time I visited Rye, I'd thought it looked like a place where Ward Cleaver would come home for a five o'clock dinner lovingly prepared by June. Even the tulips lining Main Street looked flawless—frighteningly unreal.

But that impression had been short-lived. It hadn't taken me long to discover that the fine image of this small town was all just an act of keeping up appearances. I wanted to assure Luke that Rye residents were more fallible than we appeared.

I was busy staring at Luke's shorts and imagining transgressions when he held something up. "This is for you."

I stared blankly at the object—a slightly worn canvas carrying bag, brown, with a thick blue stripe down the center—and then at Luke.

"It was Nicole's and she doesn't need it," he said, making me wonder if his wife knew he was offering me her hand-me-downs. "I'm tired of watching you struggle to carry those." He pointed to my binders.

"Thank you!" I said. I was so touched, I didn't know what else to say. I felt his eyes on me, a look I couldn't decipher.

"Here." He placed his own briefcase down, removed the unwieldy binders from my arms, and placed them in the tote. I slid the nylon straps over my shoulder and hugged the bag close to my body.

"Thank you," I said again, wondering whether I should give him a hug.

"Don't mention it," he said.

For a moment, I wondered if he meant "Don't mention it to Wim."

"So," he said, clapping his hands together and returning to business. "Let's take a look upstairs. I need you to approve the crown molding."

I started up the stairs, and he followed. My thoughts shifted from the bag to the back of my white jeans—where, I imagined, I had a ring of dirt from leaning against the dusty walls. My mother always used to caution me about buying light-colored pants: "They're hard to keep clean. And white tends to yellow over time."

Suddenly, Luke cursed loudly. He had tripped over the bottom step—the one I had recently told him protruded a bit too far into the entryway—and blood was oozing from his left big toe.

"Are you okay?" I asked, concerned.

"What architect designed those stairs?" He gave me a wry look.

"This house was built with blood, sweat, and tears," I said.

He chuckled, and I noticed his boyish smile, the way his eyes crinkled like the cellophane edges of an after-dinner mint. "Have you been sheetrocking?" he said, reaching out to brush off my shoulder, sending a cloud of plaster dust into the air. I felt blood rush through my body and my cheeks flush.

He signaled me to continue up the stairs. We reached the landing and stepped into my daughter's room.

"I love it," I said, eyeing the seven-inch strip of decorative wood hugging the vaulted ceiling. I remembered our visit to a mill one afternoon, just the two of us, to explore crown molding. The mill was bright with light pouring in through the entrance, the air thick with the scent of wood. Luke and I stood side by side, peering up at the samples of molding displayed on the walls.

It felt oddly exciting, as if we were on a first date.

Luke began by explaining the different types, how they varied in profile and size. Pointing to the displays, he said that crown molding increased the visual appeal of the walls and provided the illusion of more space. He led me to a rack and pulled out various samples. I already knew a bit about crown molding from watching *This Old House*, but I listened attentively, enjoying the camaraderie as much as the lesson in architecture. As he held each piece in his hands and pointed out the varying thicknesses and distinguishing edges, I was captivated by his reverence for what he loved.

Now he said, "I want to show you something else," and he moved to the other side of Hailey's room. He entered her walk-in closet; I stood outside the door, waiting.

"Come on." He waved me toward him.

I followed him inside.

The closet was bright, as the light was designed to turn on automatically when you opened the door—but it still felt awkward standing together in a confined space. The air between us felt warm and dense.

Then Luke shut the door behind me and everything went black.

I could sense Luke next to me and I could hear him breathe, but it was so dark we couldn't even see each other. The scent of him—woodsy and fresh, like lemons and wood shavings—stirred something inside of me that I hadn't felt in a long time. My palms started to sweat.

"What do you see?" Luke asked softly, our bodies painfully close.

"Nothing," I said, turning in his direction, my lips parting slightly. I felt a rush of anticipation and a pang of desire. My mouth went dry at the thought of him leaning in and brushing his warm lips against mine. I imagined my body pressing against his, running my fingertips through his hair and down the back of his neck. I thought I might collapse.

It reminded me of the game my friends and I had played in sixth grade—"seven minutes in heaven"—when Steve Doherty and I had stood still in the darkness in Dee Harshorn's coat closet, both waiting for the other—or for neither—to make a move. It was the first time I'd been alone with a boy, and my heart had fluttered wildly at the newness of it all. I'd wondered if Steve could hear it pounding in my chest. I'd wanted him to make a move toward me, all the while thinking, *But what would I do if he actually tried to kiss me?*

Suddenly, Luke opened the closet door. Sunlight flooded in, accompanied by reality.

Flustered, I glanced at him to see if an awkward moment had passed or if I'd just imagined it. I couldn't tell.

"Exactly," Luke said. He was standing there, looking casual, in his white shirt with the top button open, a hint of chest hair visible. "That's the disadvantage of having an automatic light. If you install mirrors on the inside of the closet doors as you talked about doing, when your kids shut the door to look in the mirror, the light will shut off and they'll be standing in the dark."

I fidgeted with the handle of my new tote, feeling both disappointed and relieved. I tried to remind myself that, just as in Dee Harshorn's closet with Steve, nothing had happened. But I worried that my face would betray me, revealing the thoughts I'd had.

Was my attraction to Luke simply lust—the kind I saw on Wim's face when he thumbed through my Victoria's Secret catalogs? Or had the demands of construction made me emotionally vulnerable?

"You don't have to do anything about it now," he said, and he began to explain how I might want to remove the automated closet lighting in the future. But I was only half listening.

"I'll have to give that some thought," I said when he was done talking. Then I picked up my bag and we exited the closet, leaving the door cracked open.

CHAPTER 30: I WANT MORE SPARKLE

Lexington Ave, Rye – January 2008

"Can we place two downlights above my bathroom vanity?"
I asked Rick, the electrician, whose eyes were fixed on the
set of electrical plans in his hands. Luke was looking at his own
notes just outside the bathroom door.

"You've got main overhead, three sconces, and a light-up
makeup mirror," Wim said, "isn't that enough?"

"I don't want shadows," I said.

Rick looked up from the plans to the ceiling and then at me.
"Vanity lights will flood the room."

"It's just . . . I want my makeup applied evenly," I said. But
that wasn't all. I'd known from the moment we decided to build
a custom home that I'd have a vanity area just like the one my
mother had had. Then, I'd stood beside her, watching her apply
peach rouge to her cheeks and coral lipstick to her lips. Now, it was

less about making sure my eyeliner was drawn perfectly and more about nostalgic longing. I wanted to recreate the bliss I'd felt as a child, watching my mom put on makeup, feeling safe and beautiful in the embrace of the bathroom vanity and her own vanity, grooming rituals that made me feel special and cared for. I wanted to be able to do it for myself, and maybe my own daughters, in our new house.

"You're not lighting a football stadium," Luke said.

"Fine," I said. But I still insisted on an additional light for the girls' bathroom when we moved on to that room.

"The girls have overhead lights," Wim said as we stood in the vanity area.

"I know. I also want one small chandelier here"—I pointed above my head—"to add some sparkle."

"Sparkle?" Wim was looking at me as if I'd asked for a small unicorn. "If you're done increasing the budget for the upstairs, can we move on to the downstairs?" he said.

I didn't let his annoyance or the five-hundred-dollar price tag on that sparkle discourage me. I was too lost in the joy and delusion of buying a glittering crystal chandelier to care.

We continued to the basement, where I told Rick the guestroom also needed more lights.

Wim turned to me, his brows furrowed. "We already have one overhead. That's enough."

"No, it's not. This room is meant for my parents, and they need more light," I said, remembering how my dad used to turn on all my bedroom lights when I studied at my desk. "Don't strain your eyes," he'd say. I shot Wim a look that said, *What's your problem?* and then looked to Luke and Rick for validation, but only Luke seemed to notice.

"How about if we buy your guests miners hats?" Luke joked.

We all laughed. But the break in tension didn't last long.

•———•

That night, Wim and I were getting ready for bed, still discussing the house. I turned to him and, though I knew it would upset him, exclaimed in frustration that our guestroom would be darker than a morgue.

"An overhead light is all that room needs," Wim said. He removed his watch and placed it on the dresser.

"It's not," I said.

Wim just stood there and stared at me. "Janie, we're talking about a bedroom that's going to be used twice a year."

"That doesn't mean it shouldn't be well lit," I snapped.

"You're being unreasonable," he said.

"No, you are," I said. "All we're talking about is extra—"

"'Extra' costs money," he interrupted. "Money we can't afford to spend."

Before I could say anything else, he'd walked out of the room.

•———•

Later, as I climbed into bed next to Wim, I felt a flicker of warmth as our little toes touched. There was a time when the slightest foot graze would have raised his antenna, but tonight, like most nights lately, instead of edging his body closer to mine, Wim turned away from me, and the only broadcast I received from him was the clicking against his teeth as he popped a plastic night guard into his mouth and fell sleep.

CHAPTER 31: THE WORLD IS FALLING APART

Raymond Ave, Rye – January 2008

On a frosty winter morning, Wim came into the kitchen after retrieving the morning newspaper, his hair dusted with snow. Plunking himself down at the table, he studied the front page of the *Wall Street Journal*, his face absorbing the dreary gray of the newsprint as he read the top headline: "US Economy Unexpectedly Sheds 17,000 Jobs as United States Slips into Recession." Somewhere between the time our roof went up and our siding was delivered, the economy had collapsed and the real estate market had tanked.

"This is exactly what I was afraid of," he said.

"What?" I asked, my mind on fabric swatches.

Wim set down the newspaper and looked at me. "The world is falling apart."

I noticed for the first time how rail-thin he looked, his once form-fitting Polo shirt now hanging loosely over his shoulders. He leaned on the table and twisted his ring. "The banking industry is in crisis, Janie." He looked at me as if to make sure I understood the gravity of the situation.

Did I? Not really. I understood the pain on his face and the severity of the headlines. But how this would impact him, and more specifically, us—no, I did not understand that. However, I knew that I had to at least try to understand in between gushing over fabric samples and obsessing about rooflines.

"I'm sorry," I said. "I know the timing couldn't be worse."

I looked out the window into the Schreibers' kitchen, where Bonnie was standing at the counter wearing an old blue house-coat that she'd probably worn since the Nixon administration. I wagered she was discussing with Maurice the same issue we were. The difference was, the Schreibers didn't have to worry about money troubles, given the small house they lived in and their modest place in Florida. Neither had we, until now.

At the height of the Wall Street boom, Wim had worked his way up to managing director and enjoyed the glory years when the market was at its peak. His lucrative career had enabled us to live well and to make some long-term investments. We had always been careful, however, to live well within our means—owning a modest home, driving inexpensive cars, and buying moderately priced clothing.

But that had all changed the day we decided to throw caution to the wind and join the flocks of Rye residents "moving up" in the housing ranks—people who, like us, felt confident that the value of their house was rising, enabling them to spend more.

My mind wandered back to my therapist's couch, where I had sat over a year earlier on a green sea of tapestry, sharing the most intimate details of my life. Linda had dark hair and a reas-suring smile and always amazed me with her ability to coax things out of me with a simple nod of her head. An hour of therapy once a week, on and off, for the past few years had been an indulgence I had allowed myself, in the hopes of becoming a less anxious and happier person.

Periodically, Wim and I had met with Linda for couple's therapy. Wim had gone willingly, though always at my suggestion. Like most marriages, ours had never been free of conflict, even before this house project.

Linda was sitting in a leather chair, her legs crossed at the knees, her lips poised in a slight, encouraging smile. There was a graceful wood coffee table between us and, as always, a box of tissues within reach.

As I looked around the office, I scrutinized Linda's décor. A small Tiffany-style table lamp sat on the corner of the oak desk. The colors of the dragonfly-patterned stained glass were deep blue and green and matched the Tibetan rug. The drapes looked like harvest gold linen, a color that added richness and depth to the room. I made a note to myself about color palettes.

"Wim and I have decided to build a house," I told her. "And we're wondering what you think."

"That's an ambitious goal," she said.

"It is very ambitious." I turned to look at Wim. "But we think we're up to the task."

"Can I ask why you're set on building a new home?" she said.

Wim and I took turns providing her a long litany of reasons— reasons we'd already spent a great deal of time discussing together at home: our need for adequate space, our yearning to create a sense of permanency in the world, our longing for a kitchen island. We viewed Linda's approval as a kind of insurance policy.

At that point, I had yet to think about my parents' approval. How their perception of me still defined me more than I wanted to admit. How I was caught between wanting to please them by living within my means yet also wanting to impress them by seeming "successful." As Linda scrawled a few notes on her note-pad, I wondered what she was writing.

"If only one of you wants this, it can breed resentment down the line," she said.

"Wim was initially reluctant," I admitted.

"I'd like to be able to retire at some point," he said.

"Can you afford to build a larger house?" she asked us. "Have you thought about what things will be like for you, financially speaking, in five or ten years?"

Wim was sliding his wedding ring on and off his finger, again and again. "It's a stretch, but we can swing it."

Linda trusted that we were reasonable people with good judgment and common sense—people who didn't make rash decisions. At least, that's what I wanted to believe.

"What's the worst thing that can happen?" Linda wasn't asking this rhetorically.

"Wim loses his job," I said. "And we have to sell our house. Cut back on vacations, music lessons, and summer camp." Just verbalizing these possibilities should have made me anxious, but it didn't. I was so secure in Wim's ability to earn a living that I never believed he might actually lose his job.

"How would that make you feel?" she asked.

I didn't want to imagine how it would make me feel. I wanted to imagine a big house with rooms to spread out in.

"If Wim lost his job? And we had to move?" I picked at a cuticle. "It would be terrible, but we'd deal with it." I knew I hadn't answered her question. But I didn't want to think about worst-case scenarios. I just wanted to get her consent, climb into bed under the covers, and snuggle up with *Architectural Digest*.

"Building a house sounds very rewarding, as long as you're not using it as a distraction from marital issues." She recrossed her legs, rested her notepad on her purple skirt, and stared at us intently.

"Things are going pretty well for us right now," I said. We were approaching our sixteen-year anniversary. Our kids were six, nine, and twelve. We were set in our routines: which side of the bed we slept on, who paid the bills, and who took out the garbage. I sometimes felt a lack of emotional intimacy with Wim that left me feeling lonely and sad, but I didn't mention that. Instead, I nodded and said, "I think we're ready for an upgrade."

•————•

As Wim and I sat at the kitchen table in silence, I couldn't stop thinking about that therapy session with Linda, wondering if she had been on to something—whether we really were using house construction as a distraction, though from what, I wasn't certain. Maybe from complacency, much like the chili recipe from my dreams that wasn't spicy enough. Or was I trying to fill a void deep in my soul?

We'd sell the house. Cut back on vacations, music lessons, summer camp. It had sounded so simple when I'd said it. Almost make-believe. We hadn't considered that the generous yearly bonus we were used to living on could become all but a memory in the blink of an eye.

I thought about my obsession over moving and how I'd insisted on getting my way, even after Wim had warned me about the economy.

And yet hadn't millions of people across the country also ignored the warning signs? If everyone was doing it, wasn't it okay?

"People keep getting laid off at work," Wim was saying, his words sounding off an alarm in my brain.

What if he really did get laid off? What if we defaulted on our loan? Couldn't pay our synagogue dues or the electric bill? I'd have to get a job—an almost laughable prospect with my limited work experience. What would I do? Work as a social worker? I'd earn less money in a week than a construction worker makes in a day. Substitute teacher? Our teenage babysitter had more earning potential than I did.

What if the bank foreclosed on the new house? Where would we go? What would my parents think?

There was no way I could tell them, not after we'd completely ignored their advice: *Always live within your means.* I couldn't bear their disappointment in me for sabotaging my family's finances and future—all because of my selfish dream. What if we had to ask my parents or in-laws for a loan? I'd sooner borrow money from a back-alley loan shark than admit to our parents that we'd overextended ourselves and needed their help.

"You've survived the cuts this long," I said.

He closed his eyes and said quietly, "I know, but I don't know what's coming next."

I'd always considered Wim the anchor in our marriage: wise, rational, in control. Now, he was a wreck. Black newspaper ink had leeched onto his fingers, and he tried to rub it off onto his palms, but it seemed no matter how much he rubbed, the stain wouldn't lift. *How could I have done this?* I thought. *If I hadn't pushed, we wouldn't be in this mess right now. We'd have a manageable mortgage, more savings, less debt.*

Outside, one of the shutters on the Schreibers' gray house hung crookedly from its hinges above Bonnie's well-tended garden. I stared at the tilted shutter; it felt almost like a personal affront, a painful reminder of our once-simple lifestyle. Meanwhile, we now had two home mortgages, two home insurance policies, two lawns to mow.

As for Wim, he'd suffered silently as he approved orders for shingles and flooring and paid invoices, watching money he'd worked for years to amass slip away, while I'd picked out fabrics and paint colors, pretending that the money spigot would never run dry.

Now that I was finally understanding the perils of debt, I began to worry about the perils of a stressed marriage, wondering how long ours could endure this kind of strain. Recently, I'd lamented over a house-related issue, and Wim's response had sounded dismissive and a little annoyed. When I confronted him, he'd said, "Then why don't you tell me what to say, and you won't be disappointed when I say it."

At times, the tension between us was so unbearable I couldn't stand to be in the same room with him.

●———●

When Wim and I were newly married, he would leave me random love notes in unexpected places, like my car windshield or bathroom mirror. The notes always made me feel cherished. But over time, those notes had become fewer and further between. So recently, when I'd reached for my pocketbook early one morning, I'd been surprised to see a Post-it note from Wim stuck to the outside pouch. I quickly read the words—*I love you honey. Wim*—and smiled.

But as my pre-coffee eyes slowly began to focus, it became clear that my brain had tricked me. The note actually read, *I took your last twenty. Wim.*

It had never occurred to me that things could actually grow this bad.

●———●

The world is falling apart. Wim's despairing words bounced through my mind like a skipping pebble. Two decades earlier, I'd stood on a cliff in Sagres, Portugal, safely ensconced in Wim's arms. "This is the end of the world," he'd said, as we looked out onto the horizon, feeling hopeful and invincible. And now here I was, his spouse of almost sixteen years, with a shamefully vague understanding of the banking crisis and how it affected him or anyone else around him, regretting my inability to help in any way.

"What do you think is going to happen?" I asked, by which I meant, *Are you going to lose your job?* On the kitchen table, my Black Book was opened to magazine cutouts of stylishly upholstered family rooms; next to it sat a grouping of fabric swatches, securely bound by a heavy metal ring, that I'd been fussing over, trying to decide which texture was best for pillows and which for sofas and drapery—a decision that moments ago had seemed so important.

"I don't know," he said. "I only know we can't afford to own two houses while my job is at risk."

I fingered a coarse swatch of linen.

"We can't wait any longer," he said.

What did he mean, we couldn't wait? Our plan was to live in this house until the new one was built. "What are you saying?" I asked.

"I'm saying we have to sell this house."

Our new house wouldn't be finished for six more months; where would we live? We had nowhere to go.

"When?" I asked. But I already knew the answer.

CHAPTER 32: NAKED AND EXPOSED

Raymond Ave, Rye – January 2008

Under a dreary January sky that threatened snow, I was waiting in line for cash at our local bank. I approached the ATM and used one hand to steady the other as I inserted my debit card into the slot. I punched in the four magic numbers, numbers that I could recite in my sleep. I held my breath and entered the command for my usual $200 withdrawal. I'd taken out cash countless times before without a second thought. But that was before a bulldozer had rolled in and crushed our newly purchased "fixer-upper," before more than a wrecking ball had hit home.

I waited for the familiar noise of bills being mechanically plucked and counted, followed by the sweet sound of the machine delivering cash. But I didn't hear that comforting whir—or see the grocery money I'd hoped would carry our family through the week. Instead, I got a message in bold print: "Sorry, you have insufficient funds available."

I slunk past the people lined up behind me, empty-handed. All at once, I realized how much easier it had been to go about life as if nothing was wrong—to deny the truth and pretend everything was fine. But here was overwhelming evidence to the contrary. Had we actually hit rock bottom?

I decided to give the drive-through a try. I drummed my fingers on the steering wheel as Michael, the teller, punched buttons on his keypad. I was sweating under my winter coat.

Finally, he looked up, and I rolled down my window, letting in a blast of freezing air. "We're sorry, Mrs. Magnolia," Michael said, making me wonder if he was apologizing for the bad news he was about to deliver or for mangling my name after I'd been patronizing the bank for twelve years, "but you can't draw cash off your overdraft protection."

"Oh." My face flushed with embarrassment. "Okay."

How could this have happened? I wondered from behind the wheel of our Honda Odyssey—a vehicle we had selected for its practicality, an exercise that now seemed laughable after all the money we'd blown on building a house.

If only we'd never left California, if only the housing market hadn't crashed, if only I hadn't decided that a new house could make my dreams come true.

I longed to return to our pre-house-building life. Where our existence hadn't revolved around an endless construction debacle. Where we hadn't struggled to pay two mortgages. Where I hadn't had to look under sofa cushions for spare change.

"Are you okay, Mrs. Magnolia?" Michael looked at me through the tinted glass window, his head tilted to the side the way our dog Copper's did when she was confused.

I started digging for something funny to say, but my humor was as depleted as my bank account. The bills were piling up at home. I'd spent the morning sorting through construction invoices and placing them in piles that stretched clear across our credenza.

"I'm fine," I said, and I thanked him for his help. Then I

pulled away in my minivan, past the leafless trees—naked and exposed—my wallet empty.

We were broke. I'd used my emergency twenty that I kept in the side compartment of my wallet that morning to pay for my daughter's field trip to Liberty Science Center. Never in my life had I not had access to cash. Never in my life had I wondered how I would pay for the backpack my son needed for school, the leotard my daughter had requested for gymnastics, or the suits Wim had asked me to pick up at the cleaners.

•———•

"We're not penniless," Wim said when I told him about the bank.

My spirits rose. "We're not?"

"No. We just have no cash." He was slumped against the couch, his head resting on an extra pillow, a glass of Coke in his hand. Normally, I'd have reminded him not to drink caffeine at this hour, but lately he'd been staying up so late each night as it was, reviewing house plans, looking over invoices, and following financial updates in the news, that it didn't seem to matter.

Wim's eyes were fixed on the evening news, the light from the TV casting a strange glow over his face that mimicked the mottled look of the grasscloth wallpaper behind him.

"The National Association of Realtors announced that 2007 had the largest drop in existing home sales in twenty-five years, and the first price decline in many, many years, possibly going back to the Great Depression," a newscaster intoned to the camera.

"What does that mean, we have no cash?" I moved from my perch on the ottoman to the leopard chair next to Wim and gripped the rolled arms.

"It means we've spent it all building this house." He looked directly at me, then down at his glass.

Spent it all? He must be exaggerating. He couldn't possibly mean *all.* I knew we had other money. "But this morning I was filing banking statements for our IRAs and CDs—"

"Those are long-term investments, Janie," he said, his jaw becoming a little tight. "We need cash. Yesterday, Brodie asked me when he could expect to get paid for the invoice he sent last month." He started reminding me of all the upgrades I'd asked for.

"You're the one who wanted to upgrade the molding," I said. It wasn't only me who had gotten carried away with spending.

"You're missing the point. I'm saying we've already used up the pot we set aside for construction. We're cashless until my bonus comes in March. Hopefully, that will cover the bills until our house sells and covers the rest."

Hopefully? What if it doesn't?

Mrs. Quigley's floodlights illuminated the yard next door, followed by Daisy's high-pitched yaps, and I knew it was ten o'clock. Soon, our own yard would light up as Wim let Copper outside one last time. Then the house would settle into quietness. Everything would be calm and peaceful again.

Except it wouldn't. Not tonight, and probably not ever.

"But I don't understand," I pressed. "We couldn't have blown through all of our savings. Can't we cash out on some long-term investments?" I felt so ignorant; I didn't even know if I'd phrased my question correctly.

Wim started talking about penalties and percentage points, and my eyes started to glaze over. *How could you let this happen?* I almost blurted, as if it were his fault and not at all mine.

This wasn't supposed to happen. We had scrimped and saved precisely so we would never find ourselves in this predicament. How naive was I? Who would ever think that on the same day that I was selecting textured chenille for my family room sofa, I'd be shaking coins from my daughter's ceramic piggy bank, searching for cash to pay for tonight's pizza?

Ever since I'd become a stay-at-home mom twelve years earlier, I'd been so absorbed with raising kids that I'd become oblivious to life outside my nucleus. My world had been reduced to Girl Scout meetings, *Goodnight Moon*, and grocery lists. Still, Wim was right. I should have paid more attention. Ever since the banking industry had begun to falter, I'd avoided the news, as if ignoring it meant it wasn't happening. I'd turned a blind eye for so long, avoidance had become my modus operandi. I hadn't realized that I could avoid facing my fears for only so long before time ran out.

I thought about how Wim had hoped for early retirement. Now, he'd be lucky if he ever retired. Only now did I stop to think about what that really meant—the continued exhausting commute, long hours, stressful job, and burden of four dependents, all his to bear.

As we sat in stillness, the only movement in the room the flickering TV screen, my gaze shifted to the built-in cherry credenza, which had been blemished with blue ink shortly after we'd renovated our home office. I'd been upset when it happened, knowing that the mark would remain there forever. I'd tried to hide it by placing a small potted plant on top of it, but I knew it was there.

I stared wistfully at the silk ivy cascading over the side of the cabinet. A leaky pen seemed a minor mishap compared to the mess we were in now.

CHAPTER 33: SUBURBAN PEEPSHOW

Raymond Ave, Rye – February 2008

On February 7, our realtor, Betsy, brought a mallet and hammered a For Sale sign down on our front lawn.

Ours was a colonial-style home, its cigar-box shape altered only slightly five years earlier when we had added on our office lean-to. The house was simple but pleasant, with plenty of curb appeal, so other than minor touch-up painting, there hadn't been much we could do to enhance the exterior. I hung a spring wreath on the door and focused all my energy on freshening up the interior. I spent a month getting our house in order, working myself into a feather-dusting frenzy, although, according to Betsy, my efforts were unnecessary.

You're your worst critic, Janie, she'd emailed. *Please don't get overwhelmed. Your house is in tiptop shape, in as perfect order as any can be.*

I couldn't be saved from myself. I wore my anxiety like a second skin under normal circumstances; simultaneously building a new house and selling an old house had wound me extra tight. If ever I'd needed a spirit animal, it was now.

Bent on making my home as clean as heaven itself, I turned to a bald white man with electric blue eyes, bulging muscles, and a penchant for tidiness: Mr. Clean. Armed with rubber gloves, a spray bottle, and lashings of tough-guy spirit, I eradicated shower mold, tackled dust bunnies under the bed, and scraped burnt blobs until my oven sparkled. I scrubbed on my hands and knees the mucky grout lines that had grayed over the years until they were restored to their natural cream color. Or had it been white?

"How did Mommy get the bathroom so clean?" my kids asked.

"Why do my toothbrushes keep disappearing?" Wim wondered aloud.

I became my own drill sergeant. My inner voice commanded me to scrub those floors and shine those faucets until I could see my reflection in them, and I listened—all the while telling myself, *We have to sell this house. We have to sell this house.* What started off as touch-up painting turned into a complete repainting overhaul; no wall was left untouched. I arranged some forsythia branches, pruned from the plant in our backyard, in a vase to bring a burst of yellow cheer indoors, and I regularly replaced them before they even began to wilt. I artfully displayed the few knickknacks we owned and otherwise freed our house of clutter. I had gotten us into this mess, and now I would do whatever I could to get us out.

The day of the realtor open house, I put out the new welcome mat my mother-in-law had given us, fluffed the pillows, placed a jar of vanilla potpourri on the kitchen counter, and prayed to the real estate gods.

•————•

"It was one of the most successful caravans I've ever seen," Betsy said. "Seventy-seven agents showed up, and they all went nuts over your house!"

Even Wim, whose praise was rare, emailed me that afternoon: *Janie, you did a GREAT JOB in getting the house together!*

Word of our house buzzed through the real estate network and, true to form, we had a flood of showings over the following days. While I was sitting at my computer one day, wondering what more I could do, I received an email from Betsy. *Is the Seller Disclosure completed? Have you selected a real estate attorney?* she wrote, raising my hopes for a quick sale. Her optimism fueled our own enthusiasm, and I imagined the thrilling conversation we would have in the coming days:

"You have three offers!" she'd say.

"They're all so good, how do we choose?" I'd ask.

"Well, there will be a bidding war and we'll see how things play out," she'd say.

•————•

The reality was that days passed without a single offer being made on our house. Days turned into weeks. The bidding war never happened. Instead, the bottom dropped out on the economy, the housing market burst, and our hope vanished.

As the weeks went by and the bills poured in, we experienced what it was like to worry about not having enough money to pay the electric bill, to not have extras like going out to dinner or my buying a new pair of shoes just because I liked them. I begged our credit card company to let us postpone payment. When they asked when they could expect payment, I didn't know what to tell them. "Soon, I hope," I said.

The FOR SALE sign I'd yearned to see on my front lawn—the message to the world that we were moving on—had become an anxious reminder that we were stuck, held captive by two houses, one that we might never sell and another that we might never finish building. We had overextended ourselves and had only each other to talk to about it. We had kept it a secret from everyone, even our parents, because we were both too ashamed to admit the risk we'd taken.

Yet, despite our challenging circumstances, I'd recently sensed a connection forming between us—a sort of "us against the world" kind of bond—as we tried to find our way out of this mess together.

"Just two years ago, houses were selling the day they went on the market. Now ours has been sitting for . . . how long has it been?" Wim asked me one March morning.

"A month," I said sourly.

Wim groaned. I could see all the stress that had built up inside him, muting the deep hazel of his eyes so all that was left in them was the last several months' mortgage payments, the landscape proposal that had come in twice as high as we'd expected, and the news that this year's bonus would be next to nothing.

Wim's bonus was the reason we lived comfortably. Wim's bonus was the reason we could move up. But regardless of Wim's bonus and whether or not we could count on it this year, Luke, Brodie, and the bank still had to get paid, making the house sale all the more urgent.

"I don't understand it. I know the market has softened, but this is a nice house." Wim sighed, sweeping a hand at the cosmetic improvements we'd made—an updated home office sheathed in trendy grasscloth wallpaper and a wall of cherry built-ins that housed a plasma TV. "Why can't we find a buyer? It doesn't make sense."

I felt like we were playing a game of hangman. Each week of no sale meant us moving one body part closer to the noose. I was convinced that by the eleventh week my hangman would appear and I would lose—on the word "foreclosure." Frustration replaced optimism, and I found myself unable to fall asleep at night, thinking repeatedly about selling the house and examining it from various angles, never making any progress. I wondered if this was where my dream died.

•———•

One afternoon, while each of us watered our side yards, I said as much to Bonnie Schreiber.

"You could always sell your new house," she offered.

I choked out a chuckle, not sure if she was serious. That night, I lay awake contemplating her suggestion.

"Maybe we should change our plan and turn the new house into a spec home, crank it out as cheaply as possible, and sell it," I said to Wim the next morning.

"It's too late," he said. "We've already poured too much money into customizing it. In this market, we'd lose even more on the new house than we will on this one."

Our situation reminded me of driving over the pointed retractable tire punctures at car-rental agencies. Once you passed, there was no turning back.

"We just have to wait for the right buyer," Wim said.

•———•

Every time the phone rang I held my breath, eagerly anticipating word from Betsy. But invariably it would be a solicitor trying to sell us something. I was tired of being hounded. The moment we'd bought the Lexington Avenue house and applied for a refinance mortgage, we'd started receiving an endless string of phone solicitations. One evening, after I'd spent the morning readying our house for show and not a single person had come, a landscaper had called. "Good evening Mrs. Margolis, congratulations on your new house! We are offering a special promotion at this time and are wondering if you would be interested in having us fertilize your lawn for only fifty-four dollars. . ."

I can't even afford the house, let alone landscaping services! I wanted to scream. Instead, I simply hung up the phone, wondering how we would finance the remainder of our home construction. I felt helpless, as if there was nothing I could do to influence the outcome.

As I stood in the kitchen, my eyes fell on the wall of plates and rested on the apple. The plate, which had been askew for months, suddenly seemed likely to fall.

•————•

I set to work on the living room window seat. It was the only thing in my house that, being Copper's guard post, was battered and scratched. I planned to brush White Dove paint over every last flaw. I strategically timed my repair work for midweek, when fewer prospective buyers were looking.

One morning, I started painting as soon as the kids had left for school, even before I straightened up the house or changed out of my pajamas. Halfway through, an agent called and asked if he could show the house in half an hour. I barely had time to finish the casing and run to my car, where I sat in my pajamas, cold and paint-streaked, until they were gone.

As I waited, I imagined potential buyers entering the house and poking through our freshly organized closets and bathroom drawers. It always felt strange to come home after a showing: a light would be turned off or a bedroom closet left ajar. These little invasions reminded me of the time burglars broke into my childhood home one summer afternoon and in broad daylight stole my mother's jewelry—her gold bracelets and cocktail rings, even her favorite pearl necklace. I remember lying still with the covers pulled up to my chin that night, my body twitching at every little sound around me—every drip of the bathroom faucet, every hiss of the air conditioner. I'd always felt safe in our house; that day, for the first time, it had occurred to me that you're never completely safe, that things can be taken away from you in a flash.

Now, my home and my family were both on display, a veritable real estate peep show. I pictured a witnessing of what brand of deodorant and toothpaste we used. I couldn't even hide the fact that I used dandruff shampoo. Anyone with an agent was free to peer into our cupboards and judge our grocery selections, criticize our snack choices. "Spray cheese! I hear that's worse for you than cocaine!" I imagined some self-righteous new mother saying.

The intruder's probing eyes would observe the intimate family portraits resting on my dresser, even my wedding photos from sixteen years ago that some of my closest friends in New York still had not seen. Betsy had suggested removing family photos from view to make it easier for the buyer to picture living in the home, but I couldn't bring myself to do it. I wanted to be private, but not invisible.

●———●

Showing our house was the ideal breeding ground for every one of my insecurities. How did I appear to the community? Did the silk living room curtains with tassel trim convey elegance or pretention? Did the trompe l'oeil mural of a window I'd had painted in our windowless powder room say clever or kitschy? I knew I was being paranoid. I knew they weren't coming to judge. But how could they not? How many houses had I walked through and criticized the architecture, even the décor, saying things I would never say if the homeowner were present? "How do you like those colors, Wim?" I remember saying as I rolled my eyes about some red and yellow stripes that lined one homeowner's family room walls like a circus tent. I knew prospective buyers would do the same thing in our home.

I also worried that they'd identify architectural features that would be deal breakers. I imagined a prospect peeking into our cramped master bathroom and saying to her realtor, "This is the master? I've seen bigger bathrooms on an airplane."

Then, one day, my fears became reality. I'd never been in the house when a buyer came to visit, but Betsy told me she'd been hearing through the grapevine that our lack of a garage (the previous owners had converted the garage into an eat-in kitchen) had turned off some buyers.

"We manage without a garage," I said. "We park in the driveway. Why can't they?"

"Not in this market," Betsy said.

Was it possible that our house might never sell?

I became so hell-bent on selling the house that my to-do list grew and grew, as if it were a kind of penance. I tried to do more and more, compensating for the lack of control I was feeling with manic perfectionism. *We have to sell this house. We have to sell this house.* Armed with a bottle of Febreze, I freshened the living daylights out of anything carpeted or upholstered, as if spraying more scent would help cover up not only dog odor and smelly boots but also the mistake I'd made in burying my head in the sand for so long.

I took a certain pride in the routine I'd established before showings: an hour before an agent brought a client to see my house, I made the beds, washed the dishes, wiped down counter-tops until they gleamed, and made sure all the toilets were flushed. I inspected each room before leaving the house to make sure each pillow was fluffed and every lamp was on so that each room took on a welcoming glow. I artfully arranged fresh fruit so the deeply purple grapes on a plate cascaded like a Monet still life. I simmered cinnamon sticks in a pot of water on the stove until a mouth-watering apple pie smell permeated every corner of the house. Then, collapsing in exhaustion but feeling high with anticipated victory, I waited. Often I sat in my minivan, parked down the street, Copper in the passenger seat, still holding on to the belief that my heroic cleaning efforts could sell our house.

• —— •

By the third week of March—just six days after Wim had received the most disappointing bonus of his career and six weeks after we'd put our house on the market—showings had slowed to a crawl and my mood had turned black. I found myself wondering why I'd bothered working myself into a state of such total exhaustion.

I sat across from Wim on the family room sofa, staring at a framed photo of our family in Park City, Utah, taken just one year earlier during a ski vacation. It was my favorite photo: the five of us leaning against a rock wall beside a covered bridge, a tall bank of white snow behind us, everyone smiling at the camera. Now I wondered when, if ever, we would be able to afford another family vacation like that one.

"I don't see any other solution," Wim was saying. He was gazing out the window at a robin returning to its nest.

"Betsy said it's the right thing to do," I said.

My teeth grazed my bottom lip as I waited for him to say something else, but there was nothing else to say. Somehow our house's continued presence on the market seemed a failure on my part, a weakness I didn't want to admit to the world. Yet I had no other option.

"I'll call her tomorrow morning," I said finally.

•———•

The next day, we lowered the price of our house.

Then we waited.

Each time our house was shown, I couldn't help but wonder if this was the one. Perhaps this was the buyer who would enjoy watching the robin family return each year to its nest in the holly tree outside the bedroom window to raise its babies. Perhaps this was the buyer who would love the way the morning sunlight transformed our yard into a gilded landscape. Perhaps this was the buyer who would revel in the neighborhood kids on the lawn together catching fireflies on warm summer nights. Perhaps. Perhaps.

CHAPTER 34: GETTING CARRIED AWAY

Lexington Ave, Rye – March 2008

One chilly day, I walked Copper with my friend Sherri, eager to show her our new house for the first time. None of my friends had seen the interior since we'd started construction.

For the past nine months, I'd hesitated to even talk about our house much for fear of being judged. Friends teased me about moving to "the other side of the tracks," implying that I would be entering a high-income, bourgeois world of hobnobbing pretension and snobbery. As if by crossing over Main Street I would suddenly become a swan of the upper class, the ultimate Park Avenue wife (albeit in the suburbs). It brought back memories of the gold-gilded faucets and crystal knobs of my youth, the big conflict of pride versus embarrassment.

Sherri and I walked up Lexington Avenue. I could see my house in the distance as we passed a large Tudor, where a homeowner stood leaning against a Lexus parked at the edge of her driveway. She was talking to a house painter, and we caught a few fragments of their conversation: "... open the beach house ... through August ... Nantucket Harbor ..."

I thought of Mrs. Schreiber's dangling shutter, her Honda Civic, a pan of homemade brownies. Would our new neighbors throw block parties on the Fourth of July? Or would they be busy opening up their houses in Nantucket? Would they help haul our water-soaked rugs to the curb if our basement flooded? Or would they just give me the number of "their guy"?

When we reached my new house, I heard heavy footsteps as Sherri and I entered the dusty foyer and caught a glimpse of broad shoulders and gray hair that I quickly recognized as Brodie's.

"I'm just tidying up," Brodie said by way of greeting. He was holding a tall broom. I remembered the laborers once telling Wim and me that Brodie liked to work beside them, sharing some of the grunt work. I was impressed by his work ethic. At the same time, I was glad that our paths seldom crossed because I found his demeanor brusque. The tension between him and Luke lately only made it worse, as Wim and I sometimes found ourselves caught in the middle of their disagreements.

"Did you see the driveway?" Brodie asked after I'd introduced him to Sherri. "We painted some lines according to Luke's drawings. One side runs right down the center of that tree at the edge of the street." He pointed in the direction of an ancient-looking oak near the curb.

"Well, we'll just have to move the tree," I joked.

Brodie didn't crack a smile. "We'll need to reduce the driveway size by a few feet," he said, reaching down to pat Copper's head. "Why don't you and Wim massage that over the weekend and let me know."

We walked him out, his heavy work boots crunching along

the construction debris. He waved a hand at the scattered fragments on the ground. "You should be careful walking around here."

His warning struck me as uncharacteristically sensitive.

Then he said over his shoulder, pointing to Copper, "She could get a nail stuck in her paw."

I lifted a hand in thanks and turned to Sherri. "Come on, I'll show you the house."

We entered the foyer and I looked around, unsure of which way to turn. I looked into the living room, at the elegant limestone fireplace surround I'd copied from *Coastal Living*. My thoughts flashed back two years to when, at the peak of my house lust, a new friend, Denise, had guided me through her newly remodeled craftsman-style home in the Township. While our youngest daughters played together in the playroom, I gazed longingly at the family room with its built-in bookcases, window seat, and stone fireplace—features I pined for in my own house—and felt a twinge of jealousy that I tried to hide under a forced smile. By the time Denise showed me her master bathroom—high ceilings, his-and-her sinks, and an oversize shower—I was so completely overcome with envy I could muster only a compliment about her claw-foot tub, the one part of the house that I knew was old. Denise had been kind and gracious, and instead of being happy for her, I'd been resentful. I'd wanted what she had, and maybe more.

Standing next to Sherri in my own foyer, I felt suddenly self-conscious, and I found myself playing down the house so as to not appear pretentious.

I tried to read her face. Was she wrought with the same sense of longing I'd felt over Denise's house? She didn't seem to be, though she did seem quieter than usual. "Let's go upstairs," I said, deciding against starting the tour with our state-of-the-art kitchen.

I led the way, but Sherri walked briskly past me as we passed through the master bedroom door. She let out a small gasp. "Wow," she said, peering around the room. Slowly taking in her surroundings—elegant French doors, tray ceiling, gas fireplace—she blinked, as if she'd entered a dim room and she couldn't trust what she saw until her eyes had become accustomed to the dark.

"We tried to create a relaxing environment," I said in an effort to sound nonchalant, though I felt my mood brighten as I remembered how Wim and I had planned the room with fastidious detail, even deciding in advance where to hang our *ketubah*, the Jewish marriage contract of our vows and responsibilities to each other that we'd read aloud at our wedding and had framed in gold. We'd chosen a wall beside the door so it would be the first thing we saw when we entered the room. Together, we'd fantasized about making our bedroom a romantic retreat.

"Imagine waking up to a warm fire and drinking morning coffee out on the balcony," I remembered saying as we studied the master bedroom plans.

"Maybe we could build a coffee nook in the corner, with an espresso machine and a small built-in fridge, so we won't even have to go downstairs," Wim said.

I shook my head and smiled. "Do you think we're getting a little carried away?"

"And whose bedroom is this?" Sherri was asking as she crossed through the bedroom into an adjacent room.

"Um—it's Wim's closet." I winced inwardly.

"This is all his?" Her mouth was agape as she glanced around a room that rivaled my childhood playhouse in size.

"Well, we had this leftover space . . ." I broke off when I saw the shock on her face.

I followed her into the connecting space—a bright, L-shaped room with two windows and a sloped ceiling.

"Which room is this?" she asked.

"This is my closet," I said. "It was unused space," I added quickly.

Her face registered no judgment, only bemused wonder.

I was looking out the window, explaining to Sherri how Luke had cleverly converted the roof eaves into closet space, when I heard another small gasp. Sherri was gone. Apparently, she had discovered the master bathroom.

"If I lived here, I'd never go on vacation," she mumbled—to herself, but for my benefit.

•———•

After the tour, we headed outside in search of the painted lines that Brodie had mentioned. As soon as I caught sight of the "driveway"—outlined in unmistakable neon pink on the existing macadam—I found myself wishing the lines had been drawn in chalk so I could erase and redraw them. What had inspired Luke to design a driveway so curved and narrow?

"Is it even wide enough for two cars?" Sherri asked.

"I don't think so," I said with a frown. "And my architect isn't going to like it when I tell him."

CHAPTER 35: ADAM AND EVE

Rosemead, CA – September 1994

The furniture in our small Rosemead apartment was a reflection of us as a couple—an eclectic collection struggling to take shape. Excited by the potential to make our new space our own, we dressed up our apartment with books, houseplants, and my dad's recycled accessories. Despite our efforts, our décor remained "early law firm." Making use of this dubious distinction, my graduate-school classmates and I once used our family room sitting area to portray an office for a mock couple's therapy session we had to videotape for a class project.

The morning of the video session, I scrambled to ready our apartment for visitors. Wim helped me dust the light fixtures, his five-foot-nine frame allowing him to access areas I could only reach with a stepstool.

An hour later, it was clean, but I still wasn't satisfied. "It looks so . . . generic," I said, trying to visualize the apartment from someone else's perspective.

"There's only so much you can achieve with paperweights and candlesnuffers," Wim remarked, unplugging the vacuum cleaner and winding the cord into a neat coil around the handle.

I knew we couldn't create red-carpet luxury on a student's budget, but I was convinced we could do better than this. "We don't even have anything on the walls. My grandma's apartment has more style than ours."

"Yeah, we should really cover our sofa in plastic too."

"At least she has real art. Our walls are so bare my friends are going to think we just moved in."

"Why do you care so much what your friends think?"

"I just want it to look nice."

Deep down, I knew Wim did too. Like me, he had grown up in a nicely decorated home—cozy and comfortable with a stone fireplace, floral upholstery, and potted orchids scattered throughout the living room. Unlike my parents' home, whose streamlined look bordered on austere, his parents' house was filled to the brim with knickknacks—picture frames, needlepointed pillows with inspiring messages ("Love Changes Everything"; "Follow Your Dreams"), and more seasonal wreaths than you'd find at a church craft fair.

But it was silly to spend too much energy on our apartment. By same time next year, if everything went according to plan, we'd be living close to the beach and the only noise we'd hear would be the ocean waves rolling off the Pacific. However, the video shoot demanded something now.

"Wait here." Wim stepped out onto the patio—our own private Eden, replete with hanging baskets, decorative plant stands, and garden ornaments. In the tiny space, we grew jasmine, raised gardenias, and nurtured the tomatoes we started from seed. Our interior design was limited by budget constraints, but our sunny exterior knew no bounds. Pots of varying sizes containing fragrant flowers decorated the small patio with rich blues, vibrant pinks, and cheerful yellows. A large trellis supported climbing morning glories, the celestial blue blossoms masking an unsightly cement wall and summoning humming-birds that hovered quietly to draw in nectar. We were proud of our garden and treated our flowers like babies—obsessively so, falling just short of carrying in our wallets two-by-three-inch photos of our precious pink petunias.

Wim grabbed our braided ficus, lugged it into the house, placed the potted tree in a wicker basket, and slid it into the vacant corner by the window. Then he went out for more plants. Within minutes, our place looked homier. I loved the ficus in particular; it reminded me of the plastic tree my mother had purchased for my grandmother's apartment long ago, the one I'd often stared at during our dinners together.

"How's that?" Wim asked.

"Better," I said. "But there's still something missing." I rolled the vacuum cleaner back into the hall closet. As I pushed it inside, something next to Wim's golf umbrella caught my eye. I reached into the dark space and grabbed the end of a mahogany-stained bamboo handle. "The oriental fan from Chinatown!" I yelled to Wim from inside the closet. The fan was the first item we had ever purchased together as a couple. "I forgot all about this!" I said, scurrying toward the futon. "We can hang it on the wall there."

"Now?"

I darted back to the closet, returned with a hammer and nail, and eyed the wall space. "Hold it up for me?"

Kneeling awkwardly on the lumpy futon, Wim unfolded the heavy paper fan until the accordion-like pleats extended into a brilliant display of delicate pink cherry blossoms, an exotic branch design with black Chinese characters on a tan background. Fully extended, it had the wingspan of an eagle.

I dashed off to grab a pencil and a ruler and returned to the sound of hammering. "I wanted to mark it first! My parents don't want a bunch of holes in the walls."

"What are they going to do, evict us?"

I folded my arms across my chest and looked at him with mock annoyance, but he was right. Our Rosemead apartment was merely a safe and controlled petri dish for how we might create a home of our own, just as our patio garden was a testing ground for how we might nurture and raise children together. One of the things I loved about my husband was how clearly he was able to see and sum up a situation.

CHAPTER 36: DON'T ASK, DON'T TELL

Lexington Ave, Rye – March 2008

One Saturday afternoon, Wim, Luke, and I met at the house to discuss construction details—things like crown molding, door paneling, and driveways. Wim and I answered question after question as we trailed Luke through the house.

"No door between your dressing area and bedroom, correct?" Luke asked.

I hesitated. *Who could remember?* These were decisions we'd made months ago.

"No door?" Luke repeated. "Agreed?"

"Agreed," we said in unison. In our state of overwhelm, we were grateful for Luke's prodding.

"I made an executive decision in the family room to remove the soffit over the window seat," he continued. "We can put it back, but I think it makes it feel more open. Agreed?"

"Agreed," we repeated. After ten months of construction, Wim and I had lost the stamina to debate details.

Wim and Luke moved on to the basement sound system. I stepped outside, where I spotted a huge box of roof shingles placed in the corner of the front porch. It reminded me that we were still a long way off from finishing the house, let alone buying patio furniture. For now, I decided, this makeshift chair would do. I hoisted myself onto the wooden container and tilted my head back to face the sun, absorbing its rays while I fantasized about summer and rocking on my front porch with my lemonade in hand.

When Luke and Wim finally made their way outside, they found me perched atop the crate.

"Careful when you get off of that," Luke said. "You don't want to get splinters in your butt."

His playful remark caught me by surprise. In some way it expressed the changed nature of our relationship, which somewhere along the line had crossed from business to friendship. Perhaps beyond friendship. I stole a look at Wim. He seemed unfazed and was laughing along with the joke. I was afraid he might suspect something, but it seemed my fears were unfounded—*And besides*, I reminded myself, *what is there to suspect?*

"Now, for the driveway." Luke turned to me. "Janie, you said you have some concerns."

The three of us gathered around the driveway—which, I noticed, was now outlined in two colors.

"So, the pink line was Brodie's *attempt* at my drawings," Luke said. "The yellow line was Vince drawing it out yesterday while I specified where it should *actually* go."

I took note of Luke's dig at Brodie. Lately, the two had had some contentious exchanges—something Wim and I found worrisome. Their disagreements could delay the project, costing us time and money.

"Angling the driveway entrance is more aesthetically pleasing," Luke explained. "It creates a nice feeling when you return home."

Driveway aesthetics had never crossed my mind. As far as I was concerned, a driveway led to a garage, and that was that. But Luke wasn't just designing our house—he was creating the *experience* of living in our home with a passion that matched our own. We'd once used the word "sexy" to describe how we wanted our house to look. Luke was trying to do that for us, and here I was, about to take the romance out of things. Still . . .

"I'm afraid I'm going to have trouble backing up," I said. "It's not easy driving a minivan; I think the driveway should be double this width."

Luke and Wim exchanged a look.

"Are you really that bad a driver?" Luke asked.

His smile told me he was teasing, but still, I felt hurt. Despite my delight over the friendship Wim had forged with Luke—a relationship that seemed to help ease some of Wim's financial and emotional stress—I envied their camaraderie. They shared many traits: an appreciation for high quality, a fastidious attention to detail, and a wry sense of humor. They respected and seemed to "get" each other. Maybe I just enjoyed Luke's attention so much that I didn't want to share it.

Sometimes I didn't know whether our individual relationships with Luke were interfering with our marriage or improving it. Luke had recently told us he'd changed his mind about placing louver lids on the front of the house.

My suggestion is to omit the louvers, he'd emailed.

Wim, who was away on business at the time, had immediately sent me a private email: *Funny, when I saw Luke's email I thought it said "lovers." I must really miss you.*

Or, I wondered, was he subconsciously worried?

When I didn't answer, Luke looked to Wim.

"No comment," Wim said.

"I'm not a bad driver," I said.

Wim looked at Luke and raised an eyebrow.

"I just think the driveway would be more comfortable for me if we widened it a bit," I said. "Besides, the area you delineated isn't big enough to play basketball on."

"Do you play a lot of basketball?" Luke asked.

My thoughts flashed to the basketball net attached to my parents' garage, my brother and me shooting hoops under the high canopies of waving, fragrant eucalyptus. My mother talking on the phone with her legs crossed and resting on her desk, my dad reclining on the family room sofa, watching an old war movie. It would not have occurred to either of my parents to play basketball with us. I thought of my younger self, longing for a stronger connection with my parents. But the memory also brought a sense of resoluteness—a determination both Wim and I felt to play an active role in our children's lives.

"I'm not looking to build a regulation-size basketball court in my driveway," I added. "I just want a place where I can spend time with my kids."

•———•

Over the next few days, Wim and I spent so much time studying Luke's revised driveway, you'd have thought we were designing the racetrack for the Indy 500. I even steered the course, pulling in and backing out over and over again until we were convinced we had a design that had just enough width and curve to satisfy all of us.

I scheduled a meeting with Luke for early Thursday evening to discuss the new design. I'll have to leave your house by eight to pick up my wife at physical therapy," he said. "But I'm all yours until then."

When Thursday arrived, Luke, armed with a red can of spray paint, set to work once again, this time with my input. By the time we finished it was dusk—the time of night when, in a few short months, the weather would warm and bats would swoop overhead. We continued working by the headlights of my minivan, a trick I had learned from Wim, who often surveyed the progress on our house in the dark, after work.

After Luke finished outlining the driveway, the two of us stood shivering in the cold, admiring our work. In the distance, evening was sounding—squirrels chattered, a dog barked, a train whistled on the other side of town.

"Finally, a driveway that looks good *and* that I can back out of," I said. I glanced at my watch. It was eight fifteen. The conversation had segued from house plans to weekend plans over the last hour, and it had felt so nice to be with Luke, to talk about things other than architecture—to get to know him better. Luke knew so much about Wim and me, intimate things like our bathing preferences and what size bed we slept in, yet I was only beginning to know him. He was smart, funny, suave—a lot like Wim. I wondered what his marriage was like. *Is he a good listener? Does he share his feelings? Do they talk about their problems?*

Lately, when it came to my feelings, Wim and I had fallen into a "Don't Ask, Don't Tell" policy, and I'd learned how to feign satisfaction. I had phoned him recently in what had become my weekly panic to tell him that, despite the eleven-foot ceiling, the beams being installed in the family room seemed to close the room in, and his response was, "You can't keep calling me and telling me you hate things, Janie. You do this every time. We spend so much time making these decisions, and then you don't even give the results a chance. I'm at work, and all I hear is worry and complaining from you . . . I just can't deal with it anymore. You're going to have to stop freaking out every time there's a change."

I hated him for getting angry with me, but how could I blame him? He was right.

Now, as I stood here having an intimate conversation with Luke, I asked myself if I was looking for something in him that I wasn't getting from Wim.

"Don't you have to get your wife at physical therapy?" I asked suddenly.

"Nicole!" His eyes widened. "I forgot to pick her up!"

I could only guess he'd been as engrossed in our conversation as I had. As he pulled out of the driveway, I caught a glimpse of him looking at me in his rearview mirror.

• ———— •

Mere minutes later, as Luke was racing to pick up Nicole and I was heading home to my kids, Wim was standing in the same spot Luke had recently occupied, tagging the driveway blue. There were so many lines, he was oblivious to the fact that in his efforts to make corrections, he was painting over the very lines Luke and I had just finished working so hard to perfect.

I discovered all this on Friday morning, when I found myself staring at what had become a confusing mess of multicolored intersecting lines akin to the old Road Atlas maps I used to carry in my glove compartment, the kind I could never refold. *It will be a miracle*, I thought, *if this driveway doesn't come out zigzagged.*

• ———— •

I arrived at our meeting with Luke the next morning bleary-eyed and carrying a college-style hangover after a night out with my girlfriends, with only a fuzzy recollection of tequila shots and karaoke in Koreatown. My last memory of the evening was staggering home from the train station with my friend Nina. Before we parted ways, the two of us stood on a street corner between our houses, attesting our love for each other. I vaguely remembered saying, "I'm so lucky to have a friend like you, Nina," and then swaying with her, our heads on each other's shoulders and arms around each other's waists, belting out "You've Got a Friend in Me."

My head was throbbing, the yard spinning. I looked around for someplace to relieve my wobbly legs, but there was no place to sit.

"Fun night out on the town with your girlfriends?" Luke grinned at me.

I grunted and plunked myself down on the asphalt, feeling embarrassed by my own uselessness.

"Do you want to discuss the driveway with us, Janie?" Wim asked.

I shook my head.

Why did I come? I asked myself. But I knew. I didn't want to miss out on seeing Luke. *What's wrong with me?* I thought as I sat there on the rough cement. *Why do I put Luke up on a pedestal?* Yet the more I told myself not to think about him, the more I did.

"We'll let her rest awhile," Wim said to Luke. I imagined Wim rolling his eyes as I heard Luke chuckle softly. The two of them stood beside me, verbally mulling over our driveway options, but my hazy brain refused to process their words.

"Janie," Wim said, jolting me out of my haze, "we decided to eliminate the front walkway and widen the driveway a little more. Are you okay with that?"

I nodded, eyes closed, stomach churning. They could eliminate the walkway *and* the driveway, for all I cared.

"I think I need to get her home." Wim took my hands and pulled me up. I felt a sudden wave of nausea; I willed myself not to throw up my buttered toast.

"Feel better," Luke said.

My eyes slowly shifted in his direction. "Thanks," I said.

I spent the rest of the day in bed with the blinds closed, my pounding head penance for my impure thoughts.

CHAPTER 37: TAKE THE MONEY AND RUN

Raymond Ave, Rye – April 2008

At 11:00 a.m. on a Sunday, the phone rang.

"Hi, it's Betsy. I just got a call from an agent in White Plains. She has a client who wants to put in an offer today."

I'd been waiting for this moment for so long, I almost couldn't believe it. I called Wim immediately to tell him the news.

A few hours later, we fidgeted in Betsy's office, ready for her to bring the deal home. Gail, the buyer's agent, strode into the room wearing a pencil skirt and a strong air of confidence. I glanced at Betsy, who, in her calico skirt, looked like she'd just walked off the set of *Little House on the Prairie*.

Have faith, I reminded myself.

Betsy made introductions, and Gail quickly took charge, explaining that the interested party was a young couple from New York City. She handed us personal letters that both the husband

and wife had separately written expressing why they wanted to buy our house. I read the wife's letter:

We love your house. We knew when we walked into your home and saw the floor plan and the beautiful deck and yard that it was the house we wanted to raise our family in.

Whether I was moved by her words or simply desperate to get rid of our house, it was all I could do not to shout, "Sold!"

Gail handed us a buyer's sheet, and we quickly scanned the document for the offer, my heart racing even faster than Gail's acrylic red nail tips were tapping the table.

It was 5 percent lower than our already-reduced price. I thought about Wim, holed up in our home office in front of his computer spreadsheet a couple of months earlier, calculating dollar for dollar our expenses against our income. "When my bonus comes at the end of March, we may be able to cover the bills until our house sells to cover the rest," he'd told me then. How devastated he'd looked when later he'd told me his bonus had been paid almost completely in company stock. The cash he'd received had been just barely enough to keep construction from coming to a grinding halt.

Wim and I returned home and lamented the low offer.

•———•

The next day, another lowball offer came in. Despite the fact that Rye's real estate market was stronger than most other regions in the nation, this new bid was off-the-charts low. My prayers for multiple offers were being answered, but they were offers we didn't want.

"Maybe we should cut our losses and take the house off the market," I suggested to Wim.

"What would that accomplish? Then we'd be stuck with two houses."

"Well, what are we supposed to do? Gail is waiting for an answer," I said.

• ———— •

Later that day, just as I'd done for the last forty-one years whenever I needed help solving a problem, I called my dad for advice.

I told him Wim and I were considering taking the first offer, even though it was lower than we'd wanted.

"Take the money and run," my dad said into the phone. But what I heard inside my head was, "We always lived within our means. You and Wim should do the same."

I felt that I was letting Dad down. If only I'd had more discipline, things wouldn't have come to this. I'd wanted to please my parents by living within our means, to impress them by living in a big, beautiful house, but I'd discovered that we couldn't do both.

"Things are only going to get worse before they get better," Dad said. "Your original price may have been optimistic, and this is not an optimistic housing market."

Though his advice sounded sensible, I couldn't help but object. "But we've already reduced the price!" I cried into the receiver. I realized I sounded like a stubborn child not getting her way, but that was how I felt.

"You're still getting 90 percent of what you set out to get," he reminded me, and he was right. My dad had a way of making everything sound so clear and logical.

"They said it was a final offer. Should we try to counter anyway?"

"You don't want to scare them off," he said. "I'd take it and be done with it."

When I hung up, I immediately called Wim. "Let's accept the offer," I said.

Minutes later, Betsy had cut a deal.

On a warm and cloudless Sunday, as the ground was finally beginning to thaw, Betsy erected an UNDER CONTRACT sign on the front lawn of our Raymond Avenue home.

CHAPTER 38: ROMANCING THE STONE

Hartford, CT – April 2008

For our sixteenth wedding anniversary, we left the kids with a babysitter and drove the ninety miles to Connecticut to complete our quest for the elusive Calacatta Gold. With our house under contract, we were feeling flush; the pending sale allowed us to resume the business of perfecting our dream house.

Gino led us through the warehouse, down a wide corridor and past the vast array of stone. I surveyed the slabs and identified them in my mind: *granite, slate, travertine*. After months of tedious research, I had not only learned the difference between soapstone and limestone; I could also tell you the country where it was quarried, its texture and grain pattern, and whether it absorbed tomato sauce.

My pulse quickened with each step as we steered closer to what I hoped would become the long-awaited surface for our kitchen island.

"Sorry, the lot you saw online last week was already sold," Gino said. "But I think you're going to like what I'm about to show you."

He didn't know that I'd been searching for months, or that in my quest for the perfect slab, I'd exhausted New York's resources and broadened my scope to out-of-state dealers.

By the time we reached the marble section, my heart was pounding a mile a minute. I let Wim and Gino converse while I gazed at the various colors and textures before me, awed and inspired by the natural wonders of the earth.

"Why has the price of Calacatta Gold shot through the roof?" I heard Wim ask Gino. It was a question I, too, had. I moved in closer, struggling to hear the answer over the din of the hydraulic machinery workers were using to move the heavy hunks of stone out of crates and onto vertical slab racks.

"It's become very popular," he said. "Granite was the boom. Now people have gotten tired of it, and the marble has been flying off the shelves. But there are restrictions on how much land can be quarried. It's supply and demand."

I was reminded of our house hunt on Lexington Avenue two years back and how the lack of availability of homes had made us want more than ever to live on that street. Classic scenario: when we can't have something, we want it more.

I followed close on Gino's heels, distracted by my surroundings. He stopped abruptly, and we nearly collided. "That's it." He gestured toward a marble slab marked "HOLD."

The sight my eyes beheld was divine: a field of dreamy white marble streaked with light gray swirls. Tiny dark spots bespeckled the cloudy swirls like stars in the night. It was just like the marble I'd seen in the pages of my home magazines, the counters that even Wim had fallen in love with. I could have gazed at it all day, but we were here to make a decision. I stopped swooning and started scanning the surface for blemishes. I glanced at Wim with a hopeful look. He raised his eyebrows; his way of communicating that the slab showed promise.

"Can we see the others?" I asked Gino.

With a commanding two-fingered whistle, he signaled a forklift operator, who quickly motored over. Gino climbed behind the wheel and maneuvered the swing boom, clamping and lifting one end of the slab. I stood rooted, my breathing shallow, as the slab rose up, reminding me of hurricane footage where huge objects like cars and trains were suddenly—freakishly—lifted into the air. I stepped back, afraid of being within the "fall shadow" of the slab.

Gino moved the forklift back and forth until he had shifted the slab far enough to the side to expose the one behind it.

"This one looks good!" I said.

Gino continued to maneuver the forklift boom, deftly moving slabs as if they were LEGO blocks, until we had selected three perfect slabs to create our kitchen island and bathroom countertops with.

"You must be a great parallel parker," I remarked as Gino came off the forklift.

"Well, I usually drive that." He nodded toward a tricked-out motorcycle in the nearby corner of the warehouse.

Wim moved toward the bike as if gripped by an external force. He pointed to a marble disk capping the muffler; it was engraved with initials, like a fine piece of jewelry. "Did you do that?"

"Yep, it's one of a kind," Gino answered.

I grabbed Wim's hand and pulled him away from the motorcycle. "We should settle up."

●———●

As we waited for Gino to write up the paperwork in his office, I thought back to the early years of our marriage, when Wim used to buy me expensive jewelry on special occasions—a diamond-encrusted heart in honor of our tenth anniversary, diamond stud earrings for my thirtieth birthday—gifts most women would kill for. I would throw my arms around him, thank him profusely, and then spend the rest of the day silently grieving over the money that could have been used toward a down payment on a bigger house.

Now, we were about to make a substantial investment in rare stone for the house I'd dreamt of back then, yet I felt slightly disappointed. I had wanted these Calacatta Gold slabs more than anything.

But maybe, deep down, I wanted something more.

CHAPTER 39: WHAT IF? WHAT IF? WHAT IF?

Raymond Ave, Rye – April 2008

R ather than wallow in disappointment, I wallowed in worry, because what concerned me more was all the things that still could go wrong with our pending sale. Though a contract agreement had been signed, we were still awaiting home inspection, and I had started remembering nightmare inspections I'd seen on *This Old House*: failing roofs, wet basements, a tire jack being used for structural support in a crawlspace. I kept turning them over and over in my mind.

"The inspector found an oil tank in the middle of our backyard," I said to Wim one morning as we got dressed. "He told me it would cost up to twenty thousand dollars to dig it up!"

"It was a dream, Janie. The inspection will go fine," Wim assured me.

"But what if it doesn't?"

I tried to remind myself that it was foolish to worry. We'd had our own inspection before buying this home. There was nothing in need of major repair. And yet . . . What if the inspector found a crack in the foundation? What if the buyer decided they wanted us to replace the roof? What if they took back their offer and the house went back on the market and we were again strapped, really strapped, for cash?

CHAPTER 40: ERECT-TILE DYSFUNCTION

Lexington Ave, Rye – May 2008

One morning, after inspecting the tile work downstairs, I headed upstairs to the master bathroom to find Leo and Stan. The two Slovakian tile installers referred to themselves as brothers, though they couldn't have looked more different: Leo was short and balding, with dark eyes; Stan was tall and fair. I'd assumed at least one of them was adopted until I came to learn that they were actually brothers-in-law.

Leo was standing in the "carwash"—his joking term for our steam shower, which was so huge I could have parked my old college Volkswagen in it (and used the multiple showerheads to wash every side of it).

Installing an oversize shower had been Wim's idea. He wanted an experience—a place he could escape into after a long day at the office and unwind with steam and a surround-sound stereo. I didn't understand the idea of bathing in what felt like a gigantic dishwasher. Why would anybody want to be steamed and come out of the shower looking like undercooked pork roll?

Leaning against the wall, eyebrows knitted, Leo was trying to make sense of a rough sketch he was gripping between grout-encrusted fingers. "This"—he flapped the wrinkled paper in my direction and shook his head—"is not much to work with." As he leaned over to set the sketch down on a plastic bucket, I detected a vague odor of cigarettes and thinset.

"I know," I said, aware how unhelpful I sounded.

He just stood there, looking at me with an expression that was somewhere between lost and frustrated. Who could blame him? I remembered looking over Joan's master bath plans with Wim the previous week; both of us had been concerned about her lack of detail. "That bathroom is going to end up being the most expensive room in the house—we can't screw it up," Wim had said.

Weeks earlier, we'd stood in the master bathroom—the three of us, Joan, Wim, and I—facing the arched window overlooking the backyard. Rays of sunshine streamed in through the trees; I'd noticed that the beech leaves had started to emerge.

Just as I'd done with Joan when designing the kitchen, I'd held my binder open to an inspiration photo, this time of an ethereal, spa-like space with pristine Calacatta marble covering every exposed surface: floors, counters, and tub surround. The marble would also be used to highlight our his-and-her mahogany vanities.

"It's going to be breathtaking," Joan had said, putting a hand over her chest.

But now, standing in the carwash with Leo, who was asking me questions about the shower walls that I couldn't answer, I realized that "breathtaking" was simply not adequate direction.

"Working with marble is different than other tile because the patterns are natural. We can either lay the tile randomly or try to line up the veining to create matching patterns," Leo explained in his charming Slavic accent as he held up one of the twelve-by-twelve-inch Calacatta Gold tiles. "It's like putting together puzzle pieces, only these can be put together in countless ways."

"What do *you* think we should do?" I asked.

He shrugged. "Marble is like artwork. Each person sees it differently."

"Well," I said, "I think I'd like the veining to flow in matching patterns. As if it were one slab." I looked at my watch. I was late to pick up my kids from school. "I'm sorry, Leo, but I have to go." I stepped out of the shower and onto crisp white marble tiles swirling with thin streaks of gray and gold; they were so fresh and pristine, setting foot on them made me nervous. "I trust you and Stan to use your artistic discretion," I said over my shoulder, the words trailing behind me.

• ———— •

Later that day, as Leo and Stan gathered their tools nearby, Luke and I stood together in the shower, eyes open wide, staring at the tiled wall opposite the shower door. An image quickly registered in my brain as . . . could it be?

Highlighted in the creamy white background, delineated in varying shades of gray, was a series of vertical lines and well-proportioned curves with the softness and openings of a Georgia O'Keeffe painting.

Luke and I exchanged a quick glance, and the look on his face confirmed my thoughts. There was no mistaking it. Smack in the center of the wall—in all its anatomical glory—was a gigantic vagina.

But that wasn't all. The vagina itself was part of a larger scene. There, in its vulval midst, standing a foot tall on either side and framing it like phallic bookends, were two unmistakable penises.

For a wild moment, I wondered whether the design might please Wim. After all, he was the one who'd been dying for a steam shower to relax and unwind in. But no; he wouldn't find this funny. His words hovered over my mind like steam that wouldn't evaporate: *This bathroom is the most expensive room in the house—we can't screw it up.*

Luke and I stood there dumbly as I wondered why Leo and Stan would do this. I couldn't have been more taken aback if Tommy, the dreamy young carpenter, had entered the shower just then, buck naked, and joined Luke and me for a rinse.

I pointed to the image, too embarrassed to name what I was seeing. "What exactly is this?" I asked Stan.

His blue eyes brightened at the question, as if he were delighted I'd asked for a full interpretation of his art.

Leo and Stan entered the shower, and as the four of us stood there—three men and me, gazing at the uncanny phallic likeness—two thoughts occurred to me: one, that our steam shower could, astonishingly, fit four adults comfortably, and two, that this situation couldn't be more ridiculous.

"You told me you wanted a pattern," Stan said, "so I followed the natural lines of the marble as they went up. It's like three candles in a row."

I looked at the "candles," two tall and bulging, the one in the center wider and outstretched, like a lemon. *Do they really not see it?* When I'd told Leo earlier that day to use his "artistic discretion," I'd never imagined that he and his "brother" would turn my shower into a *Playboy* centerfold.

How was it possible that I had another penis crisis on my hands? I was beginning to wonder if *I* was the problem. Like Freud, did I simply see sex everywhere—bolts and nuts, keys and keyholes? It's true; I saw images in the patterns of wood flooring, the swirls of paisley fabrics, the curves of connective pipes. Still, that didn't mean that every time I looked at our cupola or our shower walls I wanted to think, *penis.*

• ———— •

That weekend, I hardly slept. It was too late to order extra tile, and even if we could, it would set us back thousands of dollars. On Monday morning, I started making calls. The tile shop was closed, and Joan was on vacation for the week. I called Glenn, the operations manager, who simply gave me a philosophical lecture about prioritizing life's problems. "You have more important things to focus on right now. Besides, it's better not to disturb the tiles. The drywall may break away, and if the tile cracks, it will set the whole project back."

Finally, I called Faye, our dedicated interior designer who often went above and beyond the call of duty. Still, I couldn't help worry that even she might draw the line at penis problems.

"There's a penis in my shower," I said. "Two, actually." I described to her the "candles" and how worried I was that this was going to ruin my perfect bathroom. How Leo and Stan had no design to work from, how the tile was already set, and how this could cost thousands of dollars to fix.

"Just tell them to change it," she instructed.

"I can't," I said.

"Why?"

"Because it's a *penis!*"

• ———— •

When Faye and Leo arrived at 9:00 a.m. for our meeting, my hands were shaking so violently from nerves and caffeine tremors that riptides of coffee splashed from my cup. I had stopped by

Rye Country Store that morning and bought coffee and bagels for the painters, but unexpectedly, none had shown. Now, three coffee cups' worth of acid churned in my stomach, eating away at two buttered bagels.

"Are you okay?" asked Faye, who was pristinely dressed in a pair of gray linen slacks and a white sleeveless knit top, drop pearls dangling from her ears.

I was staring at the wall erotica, wondering how Faye would broach the subject with Leo. Still oblivious to the sexual undertones of Stan's tile work, Leo was complaining that someone had stolen his drill the previous day after he'd left it at the house.

"My client thinks the tile work is beautiful, but there are a few tiles we'd like to change," Faye began.

I glanced at Leo. His dark eyebrows frowned a little below his balding head.

Without a word about penises, Faye marked the offensive tiles with blue painter's tape. One by one, Leo replaced them with the few extra tiles we had on hand. When he was done, the genitalia had vanished, and in its place, a new image had emerged—one that Leo said reminded him of a topographical outline of old Czechoslovakia. "Maybe the mountains here." He pointed to the topside, where three peaks jutted out like a geological ridge.

Personally, I saw the San Gabriel Mountains, which reminded me of California. This was a vista I could happily look at each and every day.

CHAPTER 41: NOW WHAT?

Lexington Ave, Rye – May 2008

One afternoon, Wim and I were standing in front of the house, studying the shingle color, when out of the blue he said, "I've been bracing myself for another round of cuts at work." He stopped to take a deep breath, and then went on. "I got laid off."

A feeling of dread spread over me. "What? When?"

"Last week."

"Last week! Why didn't you tell me?"

"I didn't want to worry you."

I didn't know what upset me more, his layoff or his belated confession, but I didn't stop to question it. "I'm sorry, Wim. What happened?"

"The banking industry has changed. There just isn't a need for my job anymore." He looked and sounded defeated.

I'd been consumed by house decisions, caught up in bathroom tile, paint colors, faucets, and furnishings. Now I just felt panicky and confused. I had a heavy feeling in my chest as I looked at Wim, as if I was losing part of him.

"I'm sorry," I said again. I watched his face fall with sadness.

"Me too," he said.

We embraced and a rush of warm tears flowed from my eyes. We held each other for a long time.

Finally, I pulled back. "We're going to be okay," I reassured him.

He nodded weakly. Our mortgage payment due date was three weeks away.

CHAPTER 42: A BRAND-NEW FUZZY AND WUZZY

Raymond Ave, Rye – June 2008

On a warm Saturday morning, Wim and I found ourselves standing in our driveway surrounded by a fish tank, toddler bedding, picture books, and other possessions that had filled our home for the past decade that we'd now, like our house, outgrown. It had been hard sorting through all our things and deciding what to keep and what to sell. Some objects I'd see and immediately think, "Why did I hang on to this for so long?" Others, I couldn't let go of, especially the things that brought back happy memories. I hung on to the books I'd read dozens of times to my children and the wooden blocks we'd stacked into towers together while sitting cross-legged on the living room floor. *But why store a crib,* I reminded myself, *when a family who needs it could use it now?*

Wim and I stood facing an impatient-looking woman who seemed confused because we'd quoted her two different prices.

"Which one is it?" she asked.

"Ten dollars," Wim said.

"Excuse me a moment," I told the woman, and I pulled Wim aside.

"What are you doing?" I whispered.

"The crutches are tagged for twelve dollars. She just offered you ten, and you told her you'd take eight. You're supposed to bargain up, not down."

"Wim, they're crutches," I said. "That lady has her elderly mother sitting in the car. What if she needs them and they don't have health insurance and . . ." As I spoke, my mind flashed back to my parent's visit four years ago. They were babysitting our kids so we could spend some much-needed time alone together. Paige was napping in her crib, and when she awakened, crying, my mom ran to her—and slipped and fell and broke her kneecap. I'd felt terrible for my mother, especially because our house didn't have a guestroom and she'd had to convalesce at the Courtyard by Marriott. I was grateful that she and my dad would soon stay in our basement guest suite during their visits.

"That is not how you do business." Wim frowned and shook his head.

It wasn't how I'd have done business a month ago, when I'd felt more desperate to save every last cent possible. But now that Wim had some job prospects and we had finally closed on our house and had some money in the bank, it seemed silly to haggle over a few dollars, especially knowing what a big difference that money could make to someone else.

At the same time, I didn't want to disappoint my husband, a businessman to his core. People like Wim, who negotiated with clients for a living, tended not to be emotional about haggling. But I tended to be emotional about everything.

"I can handle this." I nodded.

"I'll be over by the bikes. Maybe somebody would like to buy your mountain bike for fifty cents," he mumbled as he walked away.

Moments later, I had sold not only the crutches but also the baby clothes, the crib, and the bassinet. I noticed a fleck of amusement in Wim's eyes, and maybe something else I wasn't used to. Admiration?

•————•

In the end, pricing didn't matter. Not many people had shown up and we'd had to practically give our things away—even the pieces with the most sentimental value, items we'd previously been unable to part with. Gone was the rocking chair in which I had nursed all three of my children. Gone was Wim's outdated but high-end college stereo equipment that he'd paid a thousand dollars for in 1988. Gone were the twin comforter and matching sheets—a circus print on a baby blue background—that we'd bought Hailey when Hunter was born. I got teary-eyed when I saw a mom and her young daughter walk away with the bedding I'd sold them. I wondered if the girl would line up her stuffed animals at the foot of the bed in descending order of size, the way Hailey had done each night at bedtime. Now she was thirteen years old and cared less about the stuffed animals she was parting with and more about the friends she'd be hanging out with in our new basement game room.

I looked forward to living in a house with plenty of space and everything brand-new. Yet, as eager as I was to move on, it was hard for me to stop thinking of this house as "home."

Ever since the new owners had agreed to rent us the house for the next month until our new house was complete, I'd been waiting with mixed emotion. Each morning when I woke up, I raised the shades and looked out over what, from now on, would be somebody else's holly tree, the same tree in which, every year, we had watched the robin family return to its nest to raise its babies, each little "fuzzy and wuzzy," as my kids affectionately named them, taking flight on its new wings. I would enjoy my mug of coffee in what was now the new owners' office and wait for that anticipated moment—it usually occurred at around 5:30 a.m.—when the sun broke through the Murrays' maple trees across the street and spilled across our yard, turning the tree-lined driveway into a luminous golden canopy.

And in the evenings, when I was ready for bed, I would climb what was now Jason and Audrey Cook's fourteen stairs to the second floor—moving as if walking on eggshells to avoid the creaking treads, having learned over the years to measure every step like an acrobat to keep from waking my sleeping children—and think of how I would miss the pencil lines we'd drawn on the kitchen doorjamb to mark the kids' height throughout the years, and how I'd miss sitting with Wim outside on our back deck, looking out at the abundant azaleas blanketing our yard.

It was with bittersweet feelings, then, that I would pack our most treasured possessions in bubble wrap—carefully wrapping our *ketubah* in protective layers and stacking swaddled picture frames in boxes marked "FRAGILE"—so we could finally move into our coveted Lexington Avenue dream house. Because deep down, I knew I was leaving a little piece of myself behind.

CHAPTER 43: SICK WITH FEAR

Raymond Ave, Rye – June 2008

Saturday was a quiet day for us. Hailey and Hunter had religious school, and Paige was at a friend's house, sleeping over.

"There you go again," I said, standing in front of Wim as he sat at the kitchen table. We'd been here before, two weeks earlier, only we'd been discussing a different aspect of the house then.

He looked up from his computer. "What did I say wrong this time?" He sounded annoyed.

"It's not what you said; it's how you said it. 'The house appraisal *has* to get done next week,'" I said, mimicking his tone. "'We can't screw around.'"

"That's not how I said it."

"Yes," I nodded. "It is."

"Whatever." He shook his head. "How I said it doesn't change the fact that we can reduce our mortgage payment by $500 a month if we refinance again and lock in this rate."

"No, but it changes whether or not you hurt my feelings."

"Jesus, Janie, I can't do or say anything to please you."

"Don't turn this back on me. You're the one who's always mad at me." I felt my eyes tearing, a lump growing in my throat. "Sometimes I think you don't even want to be with me anymore."

Before he could respond, I grabbed my purse and walked out the door.

•———•

Twenty minutes later, he found me in my Lexington Avenue closet, crying.

Maybe I was being melodramatic, or maybe I just couldn't take it any longer.

"Listen, Wim, I'm just tired of you not treating me with respect. I know things are stressful . . ."

I tried to remember how long it had been since I'd started censoring myself around Wim, monitoring everything I did or said so as not to upset him. My best guess was about a month—ever since he'd told me about getting laid off.

"Have you considered using a job recruiter?" I'd asked him one morning a week or so after the layoff as he went through stacks of insurance papers, trying to figure out how much longer we'd be covered through COBRA.

"I have, Janie. But I was a managing director. The banking industry has changed. There just aren't many jobs at that level anymore."

He looked sick with fear. His hair was grayer and thinner. His face looked gaunt, too—probably a result of the two-day liquid diet he'd had to go on after a sudden attack of colitis, an intestinal disorder that, the doctor said, could be caused by stress.

He'd found a new job now, but the stress of the past weeks had taken its toll on both of us.

Now I sat on the floor of the closet, looking up at Wim with sorrow.

"I know this is really about the house," I said quietly. "You resent me, because I was the one driving the move. I know it's frustrating for you that you won't be able to retire as early as you hoped. But you were on board too. We decided together, and now we're stuck. Maybe we should just sell the house as soon as it's finished."

"If we sell it now, we'll take a huge loss," he said; then he lowered himself to the floor across from me.

I stared at the white custom cabinets, whose Shaker style matched those in the kitchen I'd selected with Joan while designing the house eleven months earlier. "The cabinetry will last a lifetime," Joan had said.

I closed my eyes and thought about our conversation in Linda's office—the worst-case scenario exercise. Selling the house seemed like a naive solution now. I rested my head against the wall, and we sat there together in silence, the two of us lost in an enormous closet in our big "not so big" house.

It wasn't supposed to be this way. We were supposed to watch the sunrise together on our balcony, sipping steaming cups of cappuccino side by side. Our house was supposed to improve our marriage, not compromise it.

Now here we were, burrowed in the closet, facing the consequences of the decisions we'd made, good and bad.

I wanted to rewind the clock, back to the days where Wim was sitting on the couch, looking at his 401(k), and I was bathing in a tub with Fizzy Wizzies floating around me. I wanted to begin again, without all the debt we'd incurred.

"We're not building this house as an investment; we're building it to enjoy it as a place to live," Wim said, breaking the silence. "But I'm frustrated. Every day I'm on this hamster wheel, and I can't get off."

He started talking about financial planning and how much money you need to retire. He sounded like my dad. "Listen," he said, "it's not the house. I love this house. I love that you love it. I love that the kids love it. It's going to be comfortable; it's going to be home. I don't care that we put a lot of money into the house. I'm just sick of worrying about money. I worry about it every day. I worry about it when I wake up in the morning, while I'm at work, before I go to bed. I worry about how we're going to keep paying the huge taxes on this house, the maintenance, all our expenses, without me having to work forever. And I can't figure out how to do it. And it stresses me out."

I could see the stress in the set of his jaw. He looked and sounded exasperated. His words shattered me. I wanted Wim to be happy—not looking as if he were suffering from a pinched nerve. It seemed we'd spread ourselves so thin he couldn't enjoy life anymore.

I wiped my cheek on my sleeve. "I understand. I don't blame you. Something needs to change. We can't go on like this, with you stressed out and taking it out on me. I'd rather sell the house at a loss."

"Paige still has eleven more years of school. I want her to finish it out. I want to enjoy this house as a family. We'll at least wait until she graduates. But after that . . . I don't plan to pay these taxes for a school system we're not using. All I think about is when that day comes. It's like I'm wishing away time, wishing it would move faster so I can get out of this situation." His face was frantic.

I was bewildered. For as long as we'd been building this house, I'd believed Wim and I were on the same page. Though I knew he worried about our finances, he had seemed to be enjoying the project. I struggled to reconcile the Wim who had shared my fantasy of watching movies on our big-screen TV in the basement, sipping coffee on our Juliet balcony, and preparing Caesar salad in our state-of-the-art kitchen with this Wim, who was gazing at me now with a pained expression. As I sat on the floor, imagining Hailey and Hunter laughing and shooting hoops in the driveway, Paige practicing the D-major scale in the light-filled piano room, and Wim and me soaking in the Jacuzzi tub in our spa-like bathroom, I realized that I'd assumed because I was happy, he was happy too. After everything we'd been through, I couldn't bear the thought of our marriage ending over a house. Or ending, period.

"But I don't want any of this if it's going to make us miserable," I said. "I mean, I thought I wanted it. I always thought we deserved to live in a beautiful house. But not if it's a burden to us."

I'd told him this before, but now I meant it.

"It's not a burden to us, just me," Wim said.

"But that's just it, that's how you think, that you're alone in this. But you're not. I worry about money too. All the time. And I feel guilty, because it was my idea to move in the first place." Thinking back, I'd known there was risk, but I thought that if we just did it, things would work themselves out. What I'd come to realize, however, was that while you can change your mind once you've started something, the fact is, there are no do-overs in life. Only regrets.

I thought about why I'd wanted a big house so badly. How I'd been drawn in by the promise of a sense of success and security. How I'd wanted the idyllic childhood I remembered, where I believed there were no mortgages, no invoices, no burdens. How I'd thought that if I changed my environment, I could change my life. How I'd thought that if I built this perfect house, my life would look perfect—be perfect.

Now I realized that a house alone couldn't make me happy. Only the people in it could. In the end, knocking down a house and rebuilding at the top of the market during an economic crisis had only added extra worry to our lives and threatened the very sense of security I had always longed for.

"I'm sorry. I'll try to worry more with you." I smiled, hoping he would too.

He didn't, but the muscle in his jaw did relax slightly.

"Maybe we should go back to therapy," I said, half expecting him to dismiss the idea.

But he surprised me.

"Maybe we should," he said.

CHAPTER 44: LOVE ON A SAWHORSE

Lexington Ave, Rye – July 2008

On a quiet Friday afternoon, Wim and I packed Copper into the car and drove over to check on the house. It was eerily quiet; there was a noticeable absence of hammering, drilling, and sawing. The house seemed to be asleep.

The day was hot and humid. I could already feel the perspiration collecting on my lower back and sticking to my cotton T-shirt. Wim strode down the steps to the basement, the dog leading the way, while I headed to the kitchen to admire our newly installed cabinets.

The white cabinets looked crisp against the warm tones of the glass tile, a mosaic of horizontal-patterned browns and golds that contrasted with the rich, dark stain we'd chosen for the center island.

It was hard to believe that the cabinets had been installed in just one week. The father-and-son team that put them in had worked compatibly, side by side, with steady hands, as they located studs and used levels and rulers to calculate precise cabinet location, frequently checking their work against their plans. They had installed the cabinets first, the doors next; now, everything looked complete.

As I looked around the kitchen—the first room in the house to be converted from a shell to a furnished space—I felt buoyant. Despite our every debacle, our house was taking shape. There was a pot filler at the stove, a hot-and-cold water dispenser, a warming drawer—conveniences that until fairly recently I never even knew existed, let alone thought we'd own. I pictured Wim coming home late from work and sitting down to a dinner still hot from the warming drawer, us exchanging stories about our day, the kids playing together in the adjacent family room. I imagined the vibrant hum of life that would fill the air.

I touched everything, feeling the smooth surface of the cabinetry. I opened and closed every cabinet and drawer, marveling at how, with a gentle push, the drawers effortlessly retracted. Even our microwave drawer opened and closed with a single push or pull of the handle. Glancing at the range, I imagined our next holiday meal, chicken soup simmering on the stove, a brisket in the oven—the smells and memories from my childhood that we would be recreating for our own family wafting through our house, smells that turned a house into a home. Of course we'd had holidays in our house on Raymond Avenue, but this would be different; here, more of our family could be together.

"What are you doing?" Wim asked, watching me reach up to one of the upper cabinets.

"Getting in touch with my inner spackler!" My body was stretched as high as my toes would allow, my thumbnail working vigorously in an effort to extricate a stray glob of spackle.

"How about I get in touch with something else?" Wim edged in closer and gave my belt loop a playful tug, a hint of mischief gleaming in his eyes.

I ignored his advances and continued scraping my nail into the hard, plaster-like material, determined to make our new kitchen cabinets look pristine. "How about you get in touch with this spackle and help me scrape off the excess before it permanently dries onto our cabinets?" I said.

He grabbed me around the waist and slowly spun me around to face him. His hand wandered down my moist back, wedging it between me and the stove. I felt what I thought was the heat of his hand on my spine, and I suddenly realized the heat was coming from the stove.

"Wim, you turned on the burner!"

"Sorry!" he laughed.

I squinted at him. "You nearly set me on fire."

He lowered his head and raised an adorable eyebrow as if to say, *Forgive me?*

Wim knew exactly how to make me feel a little playful and reckless. The next thing I knew, he was chasing me through the dining room, up the stairs, and through our bedroom. We continued our little game of cat and mouse, cavorting like teenagers, until I found myself cornered in our two-person shower, staring at the still subtly phallic peak-and-valley veining of the marble "erect-tile," surprised to find myself slightly aroused. I sat on the freshly installed marble bench, the only flat surface upstairs other than the dusty floor, careful not to disturb the overturned paint bucket that was temporarily keeping it in place.

Wim eyed the bench uncertainly. I knew he was thinking the same thing I was—that placing double body weight on the bench was still risky. Even great sex wasn't worth a costly slab of Calacatta.

He took my hand and led me back into the bedroom, where he backed me up against a portable worktable that stood on two sawhorses in the center of an otherwise empty room.

Here? I thought, looking at thick layers of sawdust covering the table. "I don't know if this is such a good idea," I said, pressing my palm to the surface, trying to gauge how much weight it could hold.

But Wim was already arranging the twin-size plywood board. With a flick of his wrist, he whisked a leftover sheet of Tyvek paper onto the wood, covering its rough, dirty surface with the same smooth polyethylene wrap that enveloped the house—material I never dreamed we'd be using to protect our backsides. He peeled off my damp shirt, then his own. Then his shorts fell in a puddle at his feet.

"Is this—"

Before I could say "okay," my shorts were off too.

There was no graceful way to mount two sawhorses half-naked. I backed up and hoisted myself onto the tabletop, then lowered myself onto the hard surface beneath me. Wim climbed up next to me, kissing me, his lips soft and warm.

The afternoon's last rays of sunshine filtered through the dirt-coated windowpanes, lending an ethereal quality to the room. For the first time in my life, I was grateful for grimy windows and the dusty film that created a natural privacy screen from our new backyard neighbors. I was also grateful for a husband whom I loved—even more now than I had the evening we'd first been together on the not-so-private wood dock that warm summer night in Portugal so many years ago. Maybe we weren't as captivated by one another now as we once had been, but our marriage had grown in a way that allowed us to trust each other, raise our kids together, and build a house together.

I was on my side next to him, my eyes roaming over his body. I ran my hands down his back, over his arms, across his chest, almost forgetting where I was. "Tommy," I murmured softly.

Wim's eyes popped open. "Who's Tommy?"

I pointed to the letters crudely etched into the tabletop above Wim's shoulder. "It says 'Tommy' right here."

He sat up and looked at the engraving. "This saw table must belong to Tommy, the carpenter."

I sat up.

"It's fine," Wim said, leaning over to kiss me again.

"No, it's awkward."

He exhaled loudly. "Let me understand this. You'll have sex on a piece of plywood, but not if it belongs to Tommy?"

"Yes—no. I don't know." I frowned. "It's his personal worktable." I wasn't sure what I felt. Embarrassed? Guilty? Dirty?

In the midst of our bantering, approaching footsteps echoed down the hall.

I held my breath. "Did you hear that?" I whispered. "Somebody's here."

The noise grew louder and closer, and my heartbeat quickened. *Who would be here at this hour?* I wondered, horrified at the idea of getting caught naked. On top of two sawhorses.

Just as I was about to leap off the table and grab my clothes, the door that we had left slightly ajar swung open, revealing a furry mass. Copper bounded into the room, delighted to have found us. She plunked her hindquarters down beside us, cocked her head to the side, and gazed up at us expectantly.

"Out!" Wim pointed to the door.

Copper slunk away with her tail between her legs.

Then Wim's mouth was exploring the length of my neck, his sensual touch lulling me back into his powerful grip. Soon, I was oblivious to the earthy sawdust around me.

For the first time in a long while, we weren't paying attention to the house.

●———●

Afterward, we lay on our backs in the fading light, both of us staring at the tray ceiling, taking in the scent of wood and sex permeating the air. I moved toward Wim and kissed him gently on the lips, then clasped my hand securely in his. And in that moment, nestled on top of my husband's chest, feeling the steady rise and fall of each breath, I believed everything would be all right.

AUTHOR'S NOTE

This story was inspired by true events. My husband and I
built our dream house during the financial crisis and I, like
Janie, was consumed by a desire to build a perfect house. I lost
sight of reality and went on a construction bender just as the economy collapsed, making me question how much I was willing to
risk to get my dream home.

I took liberties to fictionalize the people, settings, and events
in this book because in an embellished account I could keep all the
good stuff while inventing a more heightened version of myself—
more emotional, more vulnerable, and funnier. Fictionalizing
my story also allowed me to protect people's privacy.

The cities, institutions, agencies, and stores in *As Long As
It's Perfect* are real, but I changed some characteristics and rearranged time, particularly that of the construction timeline, to suit
the convenience of the narrative. In real home construction, for
example, windows are generally ordered in the beginning of home

construction, electrical work happens before sheetrocking, painting happens after sheetrocking, and permanent stairs are installed at the end of construction, not midway through.

After twelve years of writing, fact has blurred into fiction, to the point where I often can't remember if what I wrote happened or not, and I'm not sure it matters. What matters to me is how we live our lives, and writing for me is a way of exploring the human condition.

My hope is that this story—about love and longing, money and mobility, deepened by characters who grapple with issues of image and identity in the wake of financial collapse—will resonate with readers who have had a similar experience and prompt them to consider the following questions: What does it mean to be lured by temptation? What does it feel like to lose one's financial security? What does it mean to "have it all"? What is the difference between happiness and fulfillment? Why do we try so hard to impress others? How can you be happy just being you, and not caring what others think of you?

I want the reader to connect to Janie and Wim, who, like millions of other people in America, lost their financial bearings at the peak of the housing boom and were forced to deal with the crisis that followed. I want the reader to be left feeling uncertain but hopeful about the protagonist's future, because adaption, learning, and growth, enabled by imperfection, are what allow us to progress in life, to move forward, and to succeed.

ACKNOWLEDGMENTS

I'd like to thank the people who supported me on the twelve-year journey from concept to published novel:

To my family, for their unwavering love and dedication during the tumultuous ups and downs of my book project and of my life, and for celebrating my smallest victories and tolerating my biggest freak-outs. In particular, to my husband, Chris, for being the bass to my treble, my sounding board, and my sage; there's no one I'd rather travel through the world and through life with. To my kids, Elana, Hannah, and Harrison, my gifts from the Gods, for providing tech support and moral support, and for understanding my long nights at the computer; and to my mom, Lorraine Fox (Mom, I miss you and hope you are smiling up in heaven) and dad, Harry Fox, my moral compass and my Gibraltar, for prioritizing love, family, and education. Your generosity knows no bounds. Deep gratitude to my loving in-laws, Pat and Ed Tognola, for being such a big part of our lives and celebrating milestones, holidays, and everything in between. I feel fortunate to have married into the Tognola family.

To everyone on the She Writes Press ("SWP") publishing team and their community of supportive women for believing that "women don't let women write alone": special thanks to Brooke Warner, SWP cofounder, for giving me a chance; Krissa Lagos, my gifted editor, for smoothing out my inconsistencies and making sure my tenses were perfect—and past perfect; Lauren Wise, my dedicated and patient project manager, for keeping me on track; and Julie Metz, for designing an intriguing book cover.

To my wise and earnest writing instructor, mentor, and editor, author Laura Zinn Fromm, for teaching me the elements of storytelling and encouraging me to "dig deeper."

To Jessica Wolf, for providing me with brilliant editorial assistance and keen insight and skillfully slashing my word count to save me from the fateful curse of overwriting.

To my Montclair writing group, for shouting their constructive critiques over the din of Panera Bread: Diane Masucci, Sylver McGriff, and Linda Morgan.

To my Short Hills writing buddies, for teaching me, supporting me, and inspiring me to keep going: Edna Axelrod, Jo Varnish, and Dan Kiselik. Special thanks to Dan for the encouraging pep talks; without him this book would not have materialized.

To my peeps at Women Who Write, for your ongoing friendship and support.

To my friends, for helping me to awaken and harness my humor.

To my book club, for fueling my love of reading.

To Julie Patyk, Debbie Polishook, and Cindy Slavin, for being my first readers and giving me a sense of hope.

To Lori Pine, for keeping me sane.

ABOUT THE AUTHOR

photo © Kathryn Huang

Lisa Tognola is an author, freelance writer, social worker, wife, and mother of three who always dreamed of getting married and living in the perfect house—until she discovered that passion comes with a mortgage. A former humor columnist at *The Alternative Press*, based in New Jersey, she is now a contributor to More. com and has contributed essays to five anthologies in the Not Your Mother's Books series as well as *My Funny Valentine: America's Most Hilarious Writers Take on Love, Romance, and Other Complications* and *My Funny Medical: Off the Charts Humor from an All-Star Cast*. Tognola hails from California but now lives in New Jersey, where she spends most of her time fantasizing about sunny skies, palm trees, and In-N-Out Burger.

 Lisa Fox Tognola
 @Lisatognola
 @Lisatognola

SELECTED TITLES FROM SHE WRITES PRESS

She Writes Press is an independent publishing company founded to serve women writers everywhere. Visit us at www.shewritespress.com.

Arboria Park by Kate Tyler Wall. $16.95, 978-1631521676. Stacy Halloran's life has always been centered around her beloved neighborhood, a 1950s-era housing development called Arboria Park—so when a massive highway project threatens the Park in the 2000s, she steps up to the task of trying to save it.

A Tight Grip: A Novel about Golf, Love Affairs, and Women of a Certain Age by Kay Rae Chomic. $16.95, 978-1-938314-76-6. As forty-six-year-old golfer Jane "Par" Parker prepares for her next tournament, she experiences a chain of events that force her to reevaluate her life.

Center Ring by Nicole Waggoner. $17.95, 978-1-63152-034-1. When a startling confession rattles a group of tightly knit women to its core, the friends are left analyzing their own roads not taken and the vastly different choices they've made in life and love.

Play for Me by Céline Keating. $16.95, 978-1-63152-972-6. Middle-aged Lily impulsively joins a touring folk-rock band, leaving her job and marriage behind in an attempt to find a second chance at life, passion, and art.

The Geometry of Love by Jessica Levine. $16.95, 978-1-938314-62-9. Torn between her need for stability and her desire for independence, an aspiring poet grapples with questions of artistic inspiration, erotic love, and infidelity.

Stella Rose by Tammy Flanders Hetrick. $16.95, 978-1-63152-921-4. When her dying best friend asks her to take care of her sixteen-year-old daughter, Abby says yes—but as she grapples with raising a grieving teenager, she realizes she didn't know her best friend as well as she thought she did.